# The Girl in the Blue Tie-Dye Shirt

## A Mud Street Misfits Adventure
## Book 1

By
Brian O'Dell
and
Beth Lauderdale

MUD STREET MISFITS LLC
GIG HARBOR

O'Dell & Lauderdale/Mud Street Misfits LLC
11010 Harbor Hill Drive NW #B616
Gig Harbor, Washington 98332

www.mudstreetmisfits.com

Publisher's Note: This is a work of fiction. Names, characters, places, and incidents are a product of the author's imagination. Locales and public names are sometimes used for atmospheric purposes. Any resemblance to actual people, living or dead, or to businesses, companies, events, institutions, or locales is completely coincidental.

Book cover design © 2018 Mud Street Misfits LLC

Ordering Information: Special discounts are available on quantity purchases by corporations, associations, and others. For details, contact the publisher at the address above.

Gig Harbor / O'Dell & Lauderdale — First Edition

ISBN 978-1-7326723-0-7

Printed in the United States of America

*For my Mom, Susan O'Dell*
*For always encouraging and loving her*
*little Misfit, me!*

*For Gary, who has always believed in me.*

# CHAPTER ONE

Liam led the way, with Connor close behind. He pushed downhill faster. The hulking trees lining the trail blurred in his peripheral vision. A rivulet of water from a week of heavy rain streamed down the middle of the bike trail, carving a muddy rut that Liam worked to avoid. They were almost down; one more switchback, then over the bridge and into Ashford Park. He glanced back. Connor was slipping further behind.

Connor was the natural athlete of the two— lean, wiry, and fast as a whip. But on a bike Liam's gangly body took on grace and strength, his long legs powering him up the hills and speeding him along the straightaway.

Liam felt the bike shimmy as he swept into the last curve, but he kept up the pace. The effort of pedaling through the mud, the air stinging and cooling his cheeks, the scent of blooming dogwoods and tangy pines all blended together into pure joy. When the corner unwound, Liam had the urge to stand on the pedals and pour on speed. He knew he could beat his friend to the park but instead slowed so that he and Connor could glide in together. He squeezed the brake lever and knew he'd made a big mistake. The front tire hit the sludge-coated pavement leading to the bridge. It twisted sideways, sending boy and bike skidding toward the embankment. He wrenched the handlebars and finessed the brakes but couldn't stop the perilous slide. For a moment, he hovered between control and chaos, then the bike shot over the edge. He saw the flash of sun-flecked water, the rocks lining the narrow creek, and then only darkness.

*\*\**

Pain throbbed behind Liam's left eye. The tiny circles on the standardized test form swam in his blurred vision. Gently, he massaged his temple where five stitches interrupted the smoothness of a newly shaved spot. He normally wore his dark brown hair in a retro style, bushy on top and short on the sides, but the shaved spot took the look to a new cockeyed level. He was tempted to scratch the healing cut but satisfied himself with a gentle rub.

"Thirty minutes." The proctor's voice jarred his aching head.

Four problems to go and the week of testing would be over. His mom had been mega-stressed the whole time. You'd think she was the one taking the tests. He knew that entrance into a high-ranked music school hinged on the scores, but that was still a few years away. He wished she would just chill.

His head pounded. He wanted to retreat into the bliss of orchestra class and let the tunes soothe him. It would've been nice if Mr.

Walsh had picked a different day for the dress rehearsal. He felt like his starched shirt collar had shrunk into a noose that was slowly tightening around his neck.

Shoving back the pain of the headache, he worked three of the problems, but the last was giving him trouble. He'd narrowed it down to either *A* or *C* when he realized that time was up. He filled in *C* just as the timer went off and slumped back in his chair.

"Testing's done for the year, folks. Good work." The teacher dismissed them.

Liam stood and grabbed his tuxedo jacket. As he swiveled his aching head, the room tilted and his stomach flip-flopped into his throat. He dropped the coat and grabbed for the desk like a lifeline. A hard jolt caught him in the hip and he staggered sideways into the neighboring chair.

"Out of the way, Lurch," Brandon snarled.

Liam heard Kaylee and Dylan snigger. Next came the sharp flick of a finger against the stitches and a knock to the back of his head.

* 4 *

Through the pain pinballing inside his skull, Liam watched the trio deliberately walk on the coat and laugh at the chalky tread marks left in their wake.

He sat for a moment, breathing deeply, letting his world settle. When he stood again, his feet stayed firmly underneath him. He picked up the jacket and brushed it off as best he could. Now his mom would be on his case because the coat would need to be cleaned. With a sigh, he slung his frayed red backpack over his shoulder and walked out.

Liam was halfway to orchestra class when Connor and Sarah converged on him.

"Dude," Connor said. "You have footprints on your back. Did someone walk on you?"

"Ha ha." Liam grimaced. "Just a gift from Brandon, Kaylee, and Dylan."

"Oh man. I feel your pain."

Liam remembered the disaster Brandon and his friends had made of Connor's locker and knew that he did.

"How did your last test go?" Sarah asked.

"It's over," Liam said. "That's the best part. I had a tough time concentrating."

"Ha! Maybe next time you'll listen to me." Connor punched him lightly on the arm. "I told you the key is four donuts and a Dew. That combo will keep you going."

"Oh, Connor. That's just disgusting," Sarah said.

"As I recall, you didn't do so hot on that geometry test," Liam pointed out.

Connor smirked, sweeping his tawny hair out of his eyes and tucking it behind his ears. "I didn't say it made you smart. I just said it'd keep you awake and alert."

"I don't understand how you can have the worst diet on the planet when your parents are such health nuts," Sarah said.

"Ah, that's because I know something the FDA doesn't know." Connor tapped his head.

"Oh yeah? What?"

"The foods they say are bad for you are actually the perfect things to eat. They're full of preservatives, right? Preservatives, long life. Get it?"

They stopped in front of Mr. Walsh's room, where the orchestra was already tuning up.

"You're crazy," Sarah said.

"Hah. Crazy like a fox."

"Uh-huh. Whatever."

Under normal circumstances, Liam enjoyed the constant banter between his two friends, but today the throbbing in his head made it seem as if they were talking too quickly for his brain to follow. "I don't think donuts would have helped. It's this headache. It keeps bugging me. I really wish it would go away."

"Well, no wonder, dude. When head meets rock, guess who wins."

"It's only been a few days." Sarah patted his arm. "Give it some time. Gotta get to chem lab."

"Hey, wait," Connor said. "Come over to my house after school. I have something really awesome to show you."

"Can't. I'm helping my mom at the museum tonight." She waved a hand over her head as she disappeared into the crowd of students.

"What about you, Liam?"

"Yeah, sure. What's the awesome thing?"

"Meet me at the bike rack. I'll tell you then."

Liam started to remind Connor that his bike was in the shop after being smashed last week, but Mr. Walsh's loud, frog-like voice stopped him.

"Come on, everyone. Please get settled. We have a lot of practice to do today."

"I better get in there. I haven't practiced this week because of the headache. Mr. Walsh will fry me if I mess up."

"Yeah. Later, dude."

"Nice to see you all dressed so smartly today." Mr. Walsh turned from the board as Liam made his way to where his bass stood in its stand. "I know it's been a busy week for you, so thank you for indulging me in this dress rehearsal. Now that testing is behind you, we can concentrate on the Brandenburg

Concerto in G Major. Neither Bach nor our audience would be happy if we mess up the masterpiece. Let's take it from the top, and please don't rush the notes. Keep one eye on the music and the other on me." He raised his baton. "Here we go."

As they started, Liam settled into the music like it was a favorite chair. The aching in his temple eased and the stress of testing slipped away. With every move of his fingers and pass of the bow, he slid down a path into his own peaceful world.

By the time class was over, the headache was a subdued pulse and Liam felt like he could face the rest of the day. He hefted his bass into the case and secured it in his locker.

"Liam. You did a wonderful job on the Bach piece."

"Thanks, Mr. Walsh. I wasn't too sure about the build near the end."

"Well, you played it beautifully despite your lack of practice. And that is one of the reasons I am nominating you for the Musicians Honors Performance Program."

"Really? Wow, Mr. Walsh, that's awesome."

"You deserve it. You have a natural talent and work hard. Take care of it."

"I will, Mr. Walsh. I will." He couldn't believe it. Only 100 kids were chosen for the honors program, and just being nominated was huge. A brief vision of standing on the stage at Carnegie Hall engulfed in applause made him tingle. This would be a dream come true, one he thought wouldn't be realized for years. In a daze, he floated down the hall to his next class.

\*\*\*

Liam pushed through the back door of the school to the sound of hoots and laughter. A small crowd gathered around Brandon, Kaylee, and Dylan, who were playing a game of keep-away with Connor's keys.

*Oh, no you don't.* Liam bared his teeth. Without thinking, he strode into the circle.

When Kaylee lobbed the keys to Dylan, he snatched them mid-arc.

"Stay out of this, Lurch," Brandon said. "We're just having fun with the Hobbit."

Liam spun toward Brandon, ready for battle. Pain slammed into his head. His intended charge ended in a sprawl on the dirty asphalt.

"That's better," Dylan laughed. "Now you're starting to get it."

"What's going on here?"

Liam looked through blurred eyes to see Mr. Potsroy standing on the outskirts of the circle. He was dressed in Day-Glo-orange bike shorts and shirt, holding a yellow helmet under one arm. The outfit was ludicrous, but his presence broke up the crowd. Brandon and his crew crept away.

The vice principal squatted next to Liam. "Are you all right, son?"

Liam nodded and Connor helped him to his shaky feet. "Yes, sir. I'm fine. Just tripped."

Mr. Potsroy nodded and walked away to unchain his bike. Liam watched him pedal off.

"Thanks, dude," Connor said. "If I'd lost my keys again, my mom would've given me some serious heartache."

"No problem. Just another day in the life of Lurch and the Hobbit, right?" He walked over to lean against the bike rack. "That guy is really a jerk."

"Truer words were never spoken. Maybe we should go talk to the principal?"

Liam held Connor's gaze for a minute, then they both shook their heads. "Nah. Brandon's the mayor's son and a royal butt-kisser. Nobody would believe us and it would only make things worse."

"You still up for coming to my place?" Connor asked.

"Yeah, but it has to be quick. My mom is still freaked out about the crash and wants to know where I am every second."

"It won't be. My uncle sent me some new vinyl to spin on the record player." Connor grabbed Liam's arm. "The Allman Brothers' *Eat a Peach*!"

"Nice."

"Nice?" Connor walked his bike alongside Liam. "How about 'Melissa' and 'Blue Sky'? Way better than nice."

"Yup." Liam had to agree with Connor. *Eat a Peach* was a classic. "First album released after Duane Allman passed away."

Connor nodded vigorously. "Some of the tracks are actual studio sessions that Duane did before he died. Plus, it has live cuts from their totally awesome Fillmore East gigs."

"Southern rock at its finest," they said in unison, grinning at each other.

"I need to go by my house first and check on Molly. I can't remember if my mom's working late or not. I may not be able to come over if she's not home."

***

Molly sat on the couch, still in her volleyball uniform and eating a popsicle. The sight of her legs, clad in the usual mismatched socks, stretched out on the coffee table and the blare of the TV told Liam that their mother wasn't home yet.

"Hey, Squirt, did you call Mom?"

"Nope," she said without turning away from the TV.

Liam rolled his eyes at Connor and pulled the phone from his back pocket.

"I'll be a little late today because of choir practice. Maybe an hour, hour and a half," his mom told him.

"Is it okay if I go over to Connor's house to listen to his new record?"

"Only if you take Molly with you."

"Do I have to?" Annoyance sent a stab of pain into his temple. "You know she won't want to go."

"Only if she goes with you. Got it?"

"Yeah. Okay."

"I love you."

"Love you too, Mom."

*Oh man!* He really wanted to listen to music this afternoon, but getting his sister to do something she didn't want to do was next to impossible. He sighed and shoved the phone back in his pocket. *How can I get Molly to agree to an afternoon at Connor's house?* She hated Southern rock, so mentioning the album wouldn't help. Then, he thought of the perfect lure.

"Hey, Molly," Liam said, sitting on the coffee table to block her view of the TV.

"What?"

He could tell she knew something was up. "Wanna go to Connor's with me? You can see Sadie's puppies."

"Seriously?" Molly gaped at him, the metal from her braces glinting. "Sadie had puppies?"

When he nodded, she squealed with delight and jumped off the couch, her long brown ponytail bobbing. "That is the coolest thing *ever*! When were they born?"

"I dunno." Liam looked at Connor.

Connor shrugged. "A few weeks ago, I guess."

Molly rolled her eyes. "And you're just now telling me? You guys are so lame."

"Whatever you say," Liam said, relieved that his plan worked. "I'm going to get out of this tux quickly and we can head over."

When they started out the door, Molly stopped. "Wait. I need to grab something." She ran back inside and came out with her pack on.

"What'd you get?"

"My volleyball and a treat for Sadie. I'm sure whatever you two are doing will be boring."

"Good call," said Connor. "We're going to listen to my new album and you don't have an appreciation for good music."

"Yeah, right," Molly snorted. "And, anyway, I don't want to stay too long, so don't get too wrapped up in your silly record."

***

Connor's house was a redbrick one-story that was fairly new compared to most of the homes on Mud Street, including Liam's. The garage door was open and Connor's dad was bent over behind the tool bench, digging in a bucket on the lower shelf. Molly rushed over to him.

"Mr. Harrison! Did Sadie have puppies? Liam said she did."

The man startled, rapping the back of his head on the upper shelf. The tool in his hand dropped to the concrete with a clang.

"Oh, I'm sorry," Molly said. "Are you okay?"

He grunted and rubbed the back of his skull. He looked at them, eyes huge behind dark, horn-rimmed glasses. "Hi, Molly, Liam. Sadie sure did have pups. Eight of the cutest golden fluff-balls you'll ever see." He gestured toward a wooden box in the corner of the garage. "Go have a look."

The new momma hung over the wall of the box, grinning and wagging her tail. Molly gave the big golden a hug, burying her face in the soft fur. With one hand on the dog's back, she looked into the pen.

"Oh! They are so adorable. Look at that one, Liam."

He had to admit they were really cute. One pup had separated itself from the others and was wiggling its way around the wall of the pen.

Mr. Harrison came up behind them and slung an arm around their shoulders. "You kids want one?"

When Molly shrieked, pain shot through Liam's head.

"Yes, yes! Please." She pointed to the errant puppy that had plopped itself down and was gnawing on its littermate's ear. "That one. Can I have that one?"

Mr. Harrison nudged his glasses back onto the bridge of his nose. "Only if it's okay with your mom and dad."

*Uh-oh. Now I've really done it.* No way would his mom let them have a dog.

***

Connor's new prized possession sat on his desk among piles of papers and guitar magazines. He grabbed the album and they went into the living room to fire up the record player.

The scratch of needle against vinyl echoed through the speakers and Liam smiled in anticipation. When the piano refrain started and guitar music filled the room, Connor said, "Ain't Wastin' No More Time," just like a DJ at a classic rock radio station would. He did a short air-guitar riff.

Liam bobbed his head to the drumbeat and looked over Connor's shoulder as he read the song list off the back of the sleeve.

"Look at that. 'Mountain Jam' is over thirty minutes long and takes up two sides of the record. I wonder why they put the first half on side two and the second half on side four," Connor said.

"Who knows? Because they could, I guess."

"Oh, barf," Molly said.

"Aren't you going to play with Sadie and her puppies?" Liam asked.

"Yeah, in a minute. I want to see what's so great about this album first."

Liam shook his head. He could never understand why she didn't like music the way he, Dad, and Mom did. "They did a great job with the album cover. I don't really get it, but I like it."

"What's to get? It's a drawing of a giant peach in the back of a pickup. Pretty cool, though," Connor said.

"That's too bad," Liam said, pointing over Connor's shoulder to the upper corner of the cover. Written there in blue ink was the name *Greg Ortman.*

"Yeah, but the guy took great care of his LPs. This sounds awesome and is in perfect condition."

Liam took the record sleeve and flopped down on the floor with his head toward the speakers. As the music flowed over him, he closed his eyes.

And was catapulted to a bedroom he'd never seen before. The album cover was still in his hands, but now he sat on a bed surrounded by wood-paneled walls and dirty red carpet. It smelled like week-old socks and skunk, with everything hazed over by smoke. Kneeling on the floor in front of him was a dark-haired girl wearing jeans and a blue tie-dye T-shirt. She was sobbing.

# CHAPTER TWO

L iam's eyes flew open. He bolted upright and tossed the album cover away. Immediately, he was back in Connor's living room.

"Dude!" Connor rushed to pick up the sleeve. "Be careful; this made it like forty years. I don't want to ruin it the first week I have it."

Liam jumped to his feet and staggered back a couple of steps. He shook his head, trying to clear the image of the crying girl, but even with his eyes open, he could still see her clearly.

"You okay?" Molly asked.

"I'm, uh, I'm sorry," Liam stammered.

"Dude, you look weird. Are you feeling all right?"

"I . . . I don't know." Liam sat heavily on the couch. *What the heck happened? Did I drift off and dream the girl?* He didn't think so. He could still smell the rancid smoke that had filled the room. "Oh man, that was weird." Liam touched the stitches on his temple where fire-needles stabbed.

"Does your head hurt again?" Connor switched off the stereo.

"Yeah, it does."

"Was the music too loud?"

"It wasn't the music. It was . . ." Liam shook his head.

"What?" Molly asked, joining her brother on the couch.

"When I closed my eyes, all of a sudden I was in a room with some girl." Liam shifted, feeling silly talking about what he'd seen. "She was crying."

"I don't get it," Connor said. "What girl?"

"I don't know." Liam looked into his friend's eyes. "It was just some smelly, smoke-filled room with a girl wearing a blue tie-dye T-shirt. That's it."

"You saw a girl? Just now? When you were lying on the floor with the album cover?"

Liam nodded, knowing it sounded crazy.

"Whoa, dude. That is whacked-out. Maybe you are psycho or something? Maybe the record holds some power and you unleashed it." Connor touched the album.

"First off, I hope you mean *psychic*, not *psycho*, and that's ridiculous."

"Why is it ridiculous? Maybe you saw into another world or back in time. Like in that movie, *Tomorrowland*. The girl in that could see other dimensions with the ring. Maybe this is your ring!" Connor held out the album cover.

Liam was trying to make sense of everything, but he couldn't. Trying to reason through the pounding headache was impossible. Finally, he stood up and started for the door. "I dunno. Maybe it was something I ate."

"Where are you going? We only listened to one song."

"I know, but we should probably get home. My mom will be there soon. Come on, Molly." He was relieved when she followed without a hassle. Like she knew that now wasn't the time to push any buttons.

As Liam walked down the driveway with Molly, Connor called out, "Hey, man, I'll see you tomorrow at school."

"Yeah, tomorrow." Liam waved a hand over his head without looking back. He was totally freaked out by what had happened, and he just wanted to get to the haven of his room.

***

On any normal day, breakfast for dinner was Liam's favorite meal, but tonight the smell of fried bacon mixed with the skunky smoke from his vision and gave him tilt-a-whirl stomach. He stared at the pancakes on his plate but saw only the image of the girl, tears streaming down her cheeks.

Liam's mom, Michelle, startled him back to the present by wrapping her arms around his shoulders and kissing his cheek. "Submitted for the honors program. I'm so proud of you. Mr. Walsh thinks you have a really good chance of being accepted."

"I know. He told me after class."

"You have to do a demo tape, so we'll need to pick a piece, set up a practice schedule. The deadline is only two weeks away."

Liam sighed. "Yeah, Mom. I know." He wanted to rub his temple but didn't want his mom to see him do it.

"How did the testing go today?"

"It was okay." He reached for the peanut butter and didn't look up. Maybe if he ate some food, his head would stop pounding like a bass drum.

"Liam wigged out at Connor's house. He got a headache and saw some crazy vision," Molly chimed in.

"What?" Michelle said. "What is she talking about?"

"Everything's fine." Liam tried on a nonchalant smile. "Molly's making a big deal out of nothing. Right, Moll?" He shot her a pleading look.

Liam's mom didn't say anything but touched his forehead with the back of her hand. She tilted his head so that she could look at the stitches on his temple.

"Mom, really, it was nothing." Liam shrugged off her hands.

"You sure, honey? The stitches look fine and you don't have a fever, but you don't seem quite yourself."

The last thing Liam wanted was for his mom to ask him any more questions, so he asked her one. "How was your day at school?"

She didn't answer him at first but finally said, "It was good. The group is all set for the spring concert next week. You two will like it."

"Why?" Molly asked.

"Why what?"

"Why will we like it?"

Their mom smiled and thought for a second. "Well, first off, because the choir director, *moi*, is very talented."

They all laughed and Liam was glad that he was out of the spotlight of his mom's knowing gaze.

"Secondly, it's great music from different genres. And, most of all, the group sounds amazing."

"That's cool, Mom," Liam said.

"Is Dad picking us up Friday after school?" Molly asked, shoving a large bite of syrup-and-peanut-butter-covered pancake into her mouth.

"Yes and, Liam, he'll pick up your bike from the shop on the way."

Liam nodded and the stab of pain made him immediately regret it. He was excited to go up to Black Dog Ridge with Molly and his dad, but right now, he was too distracted to really care.

"Can I be excused? I have to finish up some homework on the computer." That really wasn't true, but he was desperate to escape to the quiet of his room.

"Are you sure you're okay?" his mom asked again.

Liam forced a smile. "Fit as a fiddle. Right as rain. Nothing to worry about here." He got up from the table and cleared his plate.

*\*\**

The cursor blinked in the Google search bar. He typed in *psychic*. Part of him thought that was beyond stupid, but it was as good a place to start as any. The search came back with millions of results. Liam scrolled through the top ones: *Psychic Readings, Accurate Psychic Readings, Psychic Chat,* and *Expert Psychic Readings.* Definitely not what he was looking for.

He typed in: *What is a Psychic?* Then clicked on the link to Wikipedia.

A psychic is a person who claims to use extrasensory perception (ESP) to identify information hidden from the normal senses. The word "psychic" is also used as an adjective to describe such abilities. Psychics may be theatrical performers, such as stage magicians, who use techniques such as prestidigitation, cold reading, and hot reading to produce the appearance of such abilities. Psychics appear regularly in fantasy fiction, such as in the novel The Dead Zone by Stephen King.

He read the paragraph over until his head throbbed again. He just didn't believe in psychics and ESP. It was all make-believe mumbo jumbo. He shook his head and clicked on the link to extrasensory perception.

Extrasensory perception or ESP, also called sixth sense, includes reception of information not gained through the recognized physical senses but sensed with the mind. The term was adopted by Duke University psychologist J. B. Rhine to denote psychic abilities such as telepathy, clairaudience, and clairvoyance, and their trans-temporal operation as precognition or retro cognition. The term implies acquisition of information by means external to the basic limiting assumptions of science, such as organisms can only receive information from the past to the present.

Parapsychology is the study of paranormal psychic phenomena, including ESP. Parapsychologists generally regard such tests as the Ganzfeld experiment as providing compelling evidence for the existence of ESP. The scientific community rejects ESP due to the absence of an evidence base, the lack of a theory which would explain ESP, the lack of experimental techniques which can provide reliably positive results, and considers ESP to be non-existent.

Well, he had to admit that the image of the girl had come to him from somewhere other than the usual senses, but ESP? *Could it be? Is it possible?* It was all just too much. He kept telling himself it was nothing, but his gut said this was big and wouldn't just go away.

***

Liam had finished getting ready for bed and was listening to his go-to band, Rush. He drifted on the music, staring through the ceiling and seeing himself on the trails at Black Dog Ridge.

"Hey?" Molly appeared in the open doorway of his room, bringing him back. "Sorry about what happened at dinner."

"It's okay. At least she's still going to let me ride this weekend."

"Are you worried about it?"

"Going riding with Dad?"

"No, you know, what happened at Connor's house."

He shrugged. "Some. Yeah. I just can't figure it out." He swung his legs over the side of the bed. "I don't know what it was and I'd feel better if I did."

Molly smiled and said in her best announcer voice, "'Cause knowing is half the battle."

"GI Joe!" they said together and laughed.

"You should talk to Dad this weekend."

"Maybe," Liam said. "Just do me a favor and don't say anything to him. If I want to ask him, I will."

"Okay. G'night."

"Night."

Liam turned the light off on his nightstand and adjusted the volume on his speakers. "Fly by Night" played quietly and he tried to find himself back at Black Dog. He imagined the feel of the bike beneath him, the wind on his cheeks, but over it all was the vision of the crying girl. He was still messed up about why the vision had happened, but for the first time, he also wondered about the girl. *Why is she crying? Is she hurt . . . scared . . . what? And, most of all, why am I the one seeing her?*

***

"Dude, you are so lucky." Connor was waiting at the bike rack for the walk home after school.

"I know. I just checked the weather. The rain is going to miss us completely. It'll be perfect on the trails."

Connor was strangely quiet as they walked toward Ashford park. When he started pointing out the new buds on the trees, Liam stopped him.

"Hey, what's goin' on?"

Connor shrugged. "It's about yesterday. I didn't mean to sound like a jerk or anything. I think it'd be pretty cool if you had some special powers, but mostly I just want you to be okay."

"Thanks, man. No worries. I'm fine."

"Are you still seeing . . . you know?"

"Sort of." Liam nodded. "I did some research on the computer last night about ESP and psychic stuff. Trying to figure it out, you know."

"What did you find?"

"Nothing that was really helpful."

"Maybe you should ask the girl."

"Ha! Very funny. I just want her to go away. Have a good weekend."

Connor studied him for a minute. Finally, he grinned. "I will, but not as good as you."

Liam walked toward his house. He hadn't been completely honest with Connor. The girl in the tie-dye shirt had been in his mind all day. He'd tried to concentrate in class but couldn't push her aside. He didn't know how it was possible, but she seemed to be getting stronger.

***

His dad's tan jeep was parked in the driveway when Liam got home. The back was open and Molly was helping load their gear. Liam hurried to help. The quicker they got everything stowed, the sooner they'd be on their way to Black Dog Ridge.

"Hey, Dad."

Liam's dad, Lloyd, was a big guy, tall and sturdy. When his arms slid around Liam it was like being encased in a warm quilt. Since Liam was in middle school and grown up, he tried to avoid PDAs, or "public displays of affection," but today he held onto his dad's shoulders just a bit longer than usual.

"How's the head?" his dad asked. Just like Liam's mom had done the night before, Lloyd tipped Liam's head to the side to look at the stiches.

"It's good, Dad. No problems at all."

"Your mom said you had a headache yesterday."

"Yeah, but it's better now."

His dad studied him for a moment, then ran a hand through his close-cropped, dark hair.

"Okay. You ready to tackle the Black Dog?"

"Absolutely!"

"Well, get your gear and let's go!"

***

The hour's drive to the park was beautiful. The road wound over hills and through woods with trees so thick it was like going through a tunnel. To Liam, it felt a zillion miles from civilization and exactly the right place for him to forget about the crying girl.

As they drove by, Lloyd pointed out the sign for the cutoff to Camp Kachina. "Are you ready for camp this year? I signed you up."

"Absolutely," Molly said. "I'll be a Buffalo this year."

"How about you, Liam?"

"You bet."

"Excellent. I loved that camp as a kid. I'm glad you two feel the same way."

They drove through the park gate and paid the camping fee. A few minutes later Lloyd was pulling up to their favorite campsite along the bluff. They climbed out of the jeep.

"Man, this is so awesome," Lloyd said. "I love the view of the lake and the mountains."

"Oh yeah," Liam agreed.

"Too bad Jennifer and Jasper aren't here," Molly added.

Lloyd laughed. "Just what we need is a wild two-year-old running around the bluff and the campfire."

"It wouldn't be that bad," Molly said. "We'd all watch him."

"We'll have all summer to take them camping." Lloyd ruffled her hair. "Let's get set up and maybe we can bike down to the lake before it gets dark."

*What? Why can't we just ride now!* Liam sighed but did what his dad wanted. They got the tent up without any trouble. Once that was taken care of, Molly blew up the mats and arranged the sleeping bags. They finished it off by putting their duffle bags in the tent while their dad organized the food and coolers in the back of the jeep. All the food stayed in the car after last year when Jennifer left the Oreo cookies out and started a raccoon war in the middle of the night. The noise was horrendous and had scared them all.

"Ready for a ride?" Lloyd asked. "We can finish this up and start a fire when we get back."

"Awesome," Liam said. He lifted the bikes off the rack and handed out the helmets. His scraped a little against the stitches, but he didn't say anything in case his dad told him he couldn't ride.

Liam was so pumped he didn't wait for the others. He slung a leg over the top tube of his bike and pushed off. Electric pricks of excitement danced over his skin as he turned downhill, pedaling fast. Then, the forest path vanished. All he could see was the dark-paneled room of his vision and the sobbing girl in the blue tie-dye shirt. She loomed in front of him, bigger than ever.

His world pitched and his head spun, like he was riding the Tea Cups at Disney World. He felt a bump and the bike tipped, dropping out from under him. His shoulder hit the ground first, jarring his entire body and setting off the drumbeat throb in his temple. He groaned and rolled onto his back. Slowly, the girl faded. The tree-framed sky came into view, followed by his dad's face.

"Liam . . . buddy. Are you okay?"

"Yeah, I think so." He started to sit up. "Whoa. A little dizzy."

His dad's hands on his shoulders eased him back to the ground. "Stay there for a few minutes. Did you hit your head again?"

"I don't think so. My shoulder hurts though."

Lloyd gently lifted the arm. With one hand on Liam's back, he rotated the joint. "Is that bad?"

"No," Liam said. "Just a little sore."

"I'm sure nothing's broken, but let's get you back to camp. Do you think you can stand up?"

Liam nodded and Lloyd helped him to his feet. "Is my bike all right?"

"It's fine. Molly will come back down and get it. But you won't be riding it again for a while."

"Aw, Dad. Come on."

"Don't argue. Your mom was right. It's too soon. End of conversation."

Liam knew by his dad's tone not to push it. As they slowly made their way back up the trail, Liam was glad his dad hadn't asked him why he fell. Lloyd thought it was because of the headache and Liam was okay with that. How could he explain it to his dad, when he didn't know himself what was happening? The truth that he'd been blinded by the tie-dye girl was way weirder than just a headache.

# CHAPTER THREE

Twilight settled quickly and stars were popping out in the clear sky. Man, he loved coming out to the woods, and this was his favorite time of day.

"You guys built one heck of a fire," Lloyd said as he stuck a hot dog on the end of a sharpened stick.

They ate and enjoyed the fire, catching up on the previous week. Their dad traveled a lot for work and had been in California looking at a manufacturing plant. Liam knew that working in business wasn't something his dad enjoyed. He loved music as much as Liam did, and what he really wanted was to have his own music store, but it'd never worked out.

"Everybody ready for s'mores?" Molly asked.

"Absolutely," Liam and Lloyd answered together.

The freshly swallowed dessert churned in Liam's stomach as he wondered if he should tell his dad about the girl in the vision. *Will he think I'm crazy, or laugh at me? Which would be worse?* Finally, he took a deep breath and went for it.

"Hey, Dad."

"Yes, Liam."

"So, this strange thing happened to me over at Connor's house." Liam paused, trying to figure out how to tell his dad about the vision in a way that wouldn't freak him out. He glanced at Molly. She was nonchalantly admiring her perfectly browned marshmallow, but he knew she was listening.

"Oh yeah? What?" Liam's dad took his marshmallow out of the fire, tested it carefully with his tongue.

"Connor got this new Allman Brothers record and Molly and I went over to his house to listen to it."

"Cool, which one?"

"Uh, *Eat a Peach*."

"Nice. 'Blue Sky' is my favorite song on that LP. What's yours?"

"Well, I didn't exactly get to listen to the whole album. That's what I'm trying to tell you. This crazy thing happened."

Lloyd put his marshmallow back into the fire and gave Liam a serious look. "You got Molly to go to Connor's house and listen to Southern rock? That *is* crazy!"

Any other time, he'd love to joke with his dad. Now he just wanted to see what his dad thought of the vision. Yet he wasn't sure how to tell the story. He finally decided just to blurt it out.

"I only heard part of the first cut because when Connor handed me the album cover I . . . uh . . . kind of . . . uh . . . all of a sudden, I saw this weird vision of a girl. She was standing in a bedroom wearing a blue tie-dye shirt and she was crying. It happened really fast but was so real. I saw it all clearly and even smelled cigarette smoke."

"Huh," Liam's dad said. Carefully, Lloyd layered the marshmallow onto a chocolate-laden graham cracker and took a bite. "Perfect."

Liam waited impatiently for his dad to say something, but instead the only sounds were the crackle of the fire and the night. *How can he just sit there?* Liam didn't know what he'd expected from his revelation, but it certainly wasn't silence. The whole thing was just too bizarre to be talked about, and maybe his dad was going to ignore it. *Does he think I'm lying, joking with him?* He grabbed a small chunk of wood and hurled it into the fire.

"Dad, I'm not making this up! It really happened."

"Oh, I don't think you're making it up, Son. I'm surprised, though."

"You don't look surprised." *Or shocked, or amazed, or frazzled in any way, which is almost stranger than the vision*, Liam thought.

"Are you worried about what happened?" his dad finally asked.

"Yes . . . no . . . I don't know. It was just so real and I don't know what it means."

"What exactly is it that bothers you? Is it that you saw something or what you saw?"

"Both, I think."

"When I was eight, my grandmother, your grandma's mom, visited me in my bedroom. I was surprised to see her because nobody said she was coming to see us. She walked into the room and sat on the bed beside me. We had a nice talk about nothing in particular and then she told me she had to go and wouldn't be coming back.

"This upset me and I started to cry. I asked her why she wouldn't come back to see me, and she said that things just work out the way they're supposed to. She told me that she loved me very much. After that, she kissed my cheek and walked out of the room. I cried until I fell asleep because I loved her and knew I would miss her a lot. She was the kind of grandma who always took time to do something special with each one of us kids.

"The next morning, when I went downstairs for breakfast, my mom was sitting at the kitchen table crying. I asked her what was wrong and she said she'd just gotten a call from her sister saying that their mom had died that morning."

"Oh man," Molly breathed. "You saw a ghost!"

"No, not really. Grandma wasn't dead when she came to visit me. I'm not sure what I saw that night and I really can't explain it. All I know is that it was as real to me as sitting here with you kids right now."

"What'd your mom and dad say when you told them?" Liam asked.

"I never told them. In fact, I never told a soul until right now."

"Didn't you wonder why it happened?"

"Sure. But at the end of the day, it wasn't going to change anything worrying about it. Nothing like it ever happened again."

Liam sat quietly for a while, taking in the story. His dad's experience was unusual, but it wasn't the same as Liam's, especially the part about it not happening again. He thought about asking what his dad would have done if his grandma had kept coming back, like the girl in the tie-dye shirt was doing, but decided to drop it. He hoped she would eventually go away. If she didn't, he'd have to make her.

\*\*\*

By the time they got back to Ozark on Sunday afternoon, Liam was out-of-his-head bored. His dad had banned him from riding his bike and wouldn't let him hike by himself, either. He'd spent the morning sitting on a stump, watching squirrels play and digging in the dirt with a stick. At least he had orchestra practice to look forward to.

When they pulled up at his dad's house, Liam and Molly grabbed the duffle bags from the back and carried them inside. Jasper was playing with his trucks on the family room floor. He rushed over to Molly, arms up. She dropped her bags and swept him into the air, then pretended to drop him. It was a usual game for them and Liam laughed at the excitement on the little guy's face.

"Bubba, Bubba." Jasper reached for him. He couldn't pronounce Liam's name and "Bubba" was Jasper's way of saying *brother.*

"Sorry, buddy." Liam ruffled the toddler's hair. "Can't play right now. Gotta get to practice."

Jennifer appeared from around the corner. "Hey, guys. How was the bike ride?"

"I'll tell you later," Lloyd said.

Liam looked from his dad to his stepmom, saw the unspoken message pass between them. *He's going to tell her!* Jennifer was really nice and he liked her a lot, but he hoped she wouldn't think he was crazy.

***

Liam happily walked into the jumble of sound that was musicians tuning instruments. He felt at home here, surrounded by others who shared his love of music. After the disaster of the weekend, he needed the escape that this brought him. He carried his bass to the back of the room and positioned the sheet music on a stand. As he tuned the instrument, he sighed deeply and felt the tension in his neck ease.

"Hello, ladies and gentlemen." Mr. Walsh stepped onto the dais. "The spring concert gets closer every day and we still have one more piece to learn. I'm sure you've all studied the sheets I handed out last week and are ready to play these beautiful notes perfectly. Let's begin."

Liam let the music flow over him as he waited for his part. As it neared, he lifted his bow and placed his fingers on the strings. Pain sliced into his temple and his head rolled. He clenched his eyes shut and the image of the girl in the blue tie-dye shirt menaced into view. He choked, startled by the ferocity and detail of the vision. His fingers stuttered on the strings and the bow clattered on the tile floor. The bass slowly slid away and landed with a bang and twang of strings.

The music that had surrounded him a moment before stopped.

"Liam," Mr. Walsh said. "What are you doing?"

He opened his eyes—at least, he was pretty sure his eyes were open—but all he could see was the girl. She sobbed, shoulders shaking with the effort. The dark-paneled room from the vision blurred in the background as she sharpened in focus, lifting her from the scene like a character in a 3D movie. He could see every strand of the coffee-brown hair curled behind her pierced ear. The curve of her cheek, lightly freckled and blotchy pink from crying. The tears as they traced the line from eye to neck. Then, she began to turn her face toward him.

*Whoa, whoa, whoa!* He backed away, bumped into a stool, and heard the scrape of wooden legs against the tiles. When he felt the wall against his back, he sank to the floor. He cupped his head in his hands, and slowly, the vision faded.

Liam sat there for several deep breaths. The vision from before was bad enough, but this had been so much more intense. *Was she really turning to look at me? How is that possible? How is any of it possible?*

He realized someone was on the floor with him, talking to him. He opened his eyes to Mr. Walsh's worried look. Liam tried to smile, but it didn't quite work out.

"Liam, are you all right?"

He nodded and slowly rose onto shaky legs, grateful for the firmness of the wall at his back. "Sorry, Mr. Walsh. I just have a little headache."

"I don't think a little headache can account for what just happened, Liam. I better call your parents." He reached for the cell phone resting in the cradle on his hip.

"No." Liam grabbed the band director's arm. "No, please. Don't."

"Liam, you just collapsed. Dropping, I might add, a very expensive instrument on the floor. It's a miracle that the bridge didn't break."

"I know." He glanced at the other orchestra members gathered around. "And I'm sorry I disrupted practice, but please don't tell my folks."

"Well . . ." Mr. Walsh hesitated, and seeing a glimmer of hope, Liam rushed on.

"It's just that since the bike crash my mom's been a little freaked out. Sometimes I get a twinge in my head, but the doctor says it's normal considering what happened. I don't want to worry her anymore." Liam met Mr. Walsh's direct stare, hoping he looked more confident than he felt.

Finally, the man nodded. "Okay. I won't call them. But if anything like this happens again . . ."

"Yes, sir. I understand. It won't because I'm fine, really."

Liam picked up his bass. They both examined it for damage and Liam silently thanked whatever guardian angel might've been looking out for him that the instrument survived the fall. He started to move back to his place, but Mr. Walsh shook his head.

"I think it would be best if you sit out this practice. You can work on the piece at home. I'm sure by next rehearsal you'll have the movements down."

Liam started to object, then stopped. Maybe sitting here and listening to the music would help him figure out what to do about the girl. Rather than going away, she was getting stronger.

# CHAPTER FOUR

L iam carried a box through the garage and dropped it onto one of the tables set up in the driveway. Spring brought with it the Mud Street annual garage sale, and a stream of people walked the neighborhood, looking for bargains. His mom called it "purging time" and always came up with tons of items to sell.

"Oh good," she said. "More things."

"Yeah. I decided to sell my Tron toys and some old board games. I've almost got enough saved for the new distortion pedal. This weekend should put me over the top."

"What about Molly?"

"Don't know, but she said she'd be down in a sec."

Liam looked around at the piles, seeing everything from plastic bowls to gardening tools that'd never been used. He didn't see anything he cared about except the Christmas train. "You're getting rid of this?"

"Yup. I can't remember the last time we used it, and we really don't have room for it anymore."

He gave the train a long look. For a second, he thought about suggesting that they give it to Jasper but decided that his mom wouldn't like the idea. She wasn't too crazy about his dad's new family.

Connor walked up the driveway. "Hey, Liam. How's it going?"

"Not too bad. We have a lot of stuff this year."

"Cool. That pedal will be yours soon." Connor scanned the boxes and tables. Liam knew he was looking over the items just in case he saw something he wanted to put dibs on.

"Hello, Connor," Liam's mom said.

"Hi, Ms. MacLeod. Looks like you're going to make some money today."

"I'm more interested in making space in the house. Your family still boycotting the sale?"

"Not so much a boycott as that my dad can't part with anything. Is it okay if Liam comes with me to look around the neighborhood?"

"Sure." She put her arm around Liam's shoulders. "Thanks for your help. You guys have fun." When Molly banged through the door to the garage, she added, "And take Molly along."

Liam started to object, but his mom gave him The Look. "Come on, Molly," Liam called and started down the street with Connor, not really caring if she heard him or not.

"Let's go to Sarah's first. Her moms usually have cool stuff," Connor said.

"Hey, wait up." Molly, breathless, caught up to them. "What are you guys looking for?"

"More old records for my collection," Connor said.

"Oh, yuck."

Worried that she'd get bored and spoil everything, Liam distracted her. "How about you? Is there anything you'd like to find?"

"Yeah, a Ouija board."

"What do you want something like that for?"

"I saw a show on the Discovery Channel about them. People use them to conjure up ghosts and stuff. The full moon is coming, so maybe I can raise the Mud Street Mare."

"You're not serious? That's just a dumb story the old-timers tell."

"Nope. You're wrong. I've heard her."

"Oh, come on. You really think a horse got buried in the mud underneath the asphalt?"

"Sure. That's why they call this Mud Street!"

"My folks think the legend is true," Connor said. "Of course, they also believe in Big Foot and the UFO invasion."

"Well, I think it's crazy. And you have *not* heard a horse neighing during the full moon."

"Ha. Maybe I have and maybe I haven't. You tell me. You're the one who's psychic."

Liam looked at her sharply. *Why'd she have to go and bring that up?* He hadn't told anyone about seeing the girl all the time now and that maybe she was seeing him, too. It just seemed too weird for words.

He considered his experience with the tie-dye girl and what Molly had said. Maybe a ghost horse wasn't so strange after all.

*** 

As they approached Sarah's house, Connor slapped Liam on the arm. "Look at that."

An old, burnished-metal contraption with a shiny chrome seat stood just outside the open garage door. Connor squatted down to take a closer look. *Schwinn Airdyne* was etched into the thick metal shaft.

"Hey, kids." Sarah's mom Heather came out of the garage and set down a box of old dishes on a nearby table. She sighed with relief and rubbed her lower back with both hands. She was a tiny woman, and Liam had never seen her untidy or her hair mussed. Until today. Threads of dark hair had escaped from a clip at the back of her neck and there was a smudge of dirt on her cheek.

"Hi, Miss Heather. Where'd you get this?" Connor asked, pointing to the bike.

"Oh, Rachel picked it up at a flea market a few months ago." Heather laughed softly. "One of those things she knew I couldn't live without." She patted the seat affectionately. "I do love it, but I just don't have any more room."

"It's pretty cool. How does it work?"

"Jump on and I'll show you."

Connor climbed onto the seat and grabbed the handlebars. As he started to pedal, the handlebars moved forward and back so that he looked like he was riding a slow-moving bucking bronco. It seemed easy at first. Then Heather placed her hand on a small dial and started to turn it. The more she turned, the harder it was for Connor to move. He was pushing and pedaling as hard as he could, but he was slowing with each turn. She turned the dial until Connor could no longer move the machine and he came to a stop.

"Wow, that's hard," Connor said. "Is that all it does?"

"Yep. It's an antique exercise machine. Early forerunner to the stationary bike."

"I don't really get those. Why wouldn't you just ride a normal bike?"

"I guess if the weather's bad and you can't go outside, you can still get exercise. Like a treadmill, but for biking."

"I think they're cool," Molly said. "You could bike and watch TV at the same time!"

"You sure could, Molly," Heather agreed. "Sarah's inside. I'll let her know you're here. Look around if you want to."

She went back into the house and Connor beelined for the books and magazines. Molly pulled an old badminton racquet out of a big wooden box and swooshed it through the air.

Liam stood for a moment with his hand on the seat of the exercycle and then spotted an old school desk. He walked over to take a closer look. It was small, the wooden top pitted from years of use and carved with dozens of initials. The metal legs were bent and streaked with rust.

He knelt down and laid his hand on the top of the desk. Instantly, he was in the middle of a storm. Lightning flashed and thunder boomed around him. Windows shattered and a banshee wind shrieked in. Children screamed. Grit pelted his face and he ducked as shards of glass and splinters of wood flew by his head. A sudden blast tore the desk from beneath his hand. It shot through the air and slammed against the wall.

Liam jerked his hand away. *Oh no. Not again.* His head pounded and he thought he might barf. *Am I losing my mind? Growing a massive brain tumor?* It was bad enough having the tie-dye girl in his face all the time. *Is it going to happen with everything I touch?* Slowly, he stood and took some deep breaths.

Something bumped his arm. He jumped and spun around.

"Hey. Wow. Sorry." Heather held up a hand. "I didn't mean to startle you." She was carrying a rusty bird cage and gently set it on the ground. "Cool old desk, isn't it?"

"Oh . . . uh . . . yeah."

"It's been through a lot. I found it in a ramshackle barn near Springfield. The man I bought it from said that it was from an old schoolhouse down in Alma. He went there to help clean up after the big tornado a few years ago." She shook her head. "I only saw pictures on TV, but he said that the town was a real mess. People who'd lived there all their lives left with nothing. Lots of buildings ruined. The school was demolished. Good thing no kids were seriously hurt. Anyway, he thought he could do something with this old thing, but never did. I bought it because I loved the history of it. Now, I have no idea what I'll do with it. You want it?"

Liam backed away. "Er . . . thanks, Miss Heather, but no." He walked quickly down the driveway. Vaguely, he heard Sarah and Connor shouting at him, but he kept going.

"Hey, what's up?" Connor asked, falling in next to him, with Molly and Sarah on the other side.

"Nothing, I just need to get home," Liam said, staring straight ahead. He just wanted to get to his room, maybe hide under the bed or in the closet.

"But we didn't even make it halfway down the street," Molly whined.

Liam stopped and turned to them. "It happened again."

"What happened again?"

"IT!"

"Oh man," Connor whispered. "Another vision?"

"Yes," Liam said. He bit his lip to keep from telling them the rest of it.

"It? Vision? What're you talking about?" Sarah stared at them.

"Top secret stuff," Connor said. "We may need to be by ourselves"

"Jeez," Sarah said. "If you girls need to be alone, I'm out of here."

"Knock it off, Connor," Liam said and poked him in the side. "Don't pay any attention to him, Sarah." He rubbed a hand across his cheek where the dirt had peppered his skin. "I just need to get home, then maybe I can talk about it." *But what am I going say? That I think I'm going crazy? Ask where the closest loony bin is?*

# CHAPTER FIVE

They were almost to Liam's house when Connor grabbed his arm. "Let's go to my place. My folks are shopping for a new juicer and we'll have the house to ourselves."

Liam hesitated. The thought of retreating to his room seemed like such a good idea. But he really didn't want to talk to his mom right now and he knew she would wonder why he'd come home early.

Connor used his key to let them in and they went straight to the living room. Liam threw himself into the leather chair where Connor's dad always sat. He could feel three pairs of eyes on him and he knew they were waiting for him to tell them what had happened. *How do you start a conversation like this?* He had no idea and almost laughed at the weirdness of it.

"Connor, can I have a Coke?"

"Dude, did you forget where you are? This house has never had a Coke in it." Connor went into the kitchen. "We have Oogave Citrus Paradisi organic soda. And in case you're worried, there are no GMOs in it."

"That's fine. Whatever."

Connor grabbed four and passed them out. Liam popped the top on his and took a big gulp. He didn't stop the burp that followed and was glad when Connor laughed. His concern about spilling his guts eased a bit. Even if this was the last conversation he had before he was committed for insanity, at least he'd enjoy it with his friends.

"This actually isn't that bad," Connor said after a sip. "It is not that good, either. Kind of blah."

"So, what is *It*, Liam? What's going on?" Sarah asked, sinking to the floor to sit cross-legged.

"It all starts with Greg Ortman and the *Eat a Peach* album," Liam said.

"It's a classic rock album that my uncle gave me. Greg Ortman is written on the sleeve," Connor told her.

"Is it a first and last name?"

"I think so," Liam replied.

"So, what's the big deal?"

"That's the top secret part," Connor said and glanced at Liam.

Sarah narrowed her eyes. "What are you up to?" When they didn't answer, she turned to Molly. "Are you in on this, too?"

"Kind of," Molly said, looking a little sheepish.

Liam took a deep breath and looked at Connor. "I'm going to tell her."

"You sure?"

"Yes. Besides, she may be able to help. Can you keep a secret?" Liam looked at Sarah.

"It depends. How much trouble are we going to get into for this?"

"Hopefully none, but no guarantees."

"Good enough for me."

Liam started from the beginning and told Sarah everything that'd happened with the album.

"And, now, the girl keeps coming back, whether I'm holding the album or not. It's like she's stuck to me or something."

"Is that why you crashed your bike last weekend?" Molly asked.

Liam nodded. "And she's bigger every time. I swear, last time, during orchestra practice, she moved. Almost like she was turning toward me."

"What? Liam, you realize that sounds crazy, right?" Sarah asked.

"Duh. That's why I didn't want anyone to know about this. It just happened again with that old desk . . . When I touched it, I felt like I was in this wild windstorm or something. It was loud and dark. Dirt blew all around me. Then, I think the roof ripped off the building or maybe it blew up, I don't know, but the desk just ripped out from under my hand and flew against the wall. It was bizarre . . . intense, but it only lasted a second or two." He took another swig of his organic soda. "Then your mom comes up and tells me that the desk had been in a tornado down in Alma."

"Wow," Molly whispered.

"This *is* amazing!" Connor jumped up, pacing back and forth. "I tell you, this is awesome. I'm not sure why yet, but Liam, this is the coolest thing ever. You have some sort of superpower."

"What's so great about it?" Liam looked at Connor. "I can't play my bass. I can't ride my bike. The tie-dye girl is ruining my life."

"Dude! Are you kidding me? With just a touch, you were able to see into the past . . . or the future, whatever. Do you know anyone else who can do that? I sure don't. Well, until now. Liam, I'm telling you, this is awesome."

"Heck, yeah." Molly shot off the couch. "He's right. Liam. You're, like, psychic or something."

Liam looked from his friends to his sister. "I don't know, guys. It's all just too weird.

Who is this guy, Ortman? Who's the girl? Why is she crying? What's she frightened of? And . . . why me?"

"Well, first of all, why not you?" Connor asked.

"He's right," Sarah agreed. "Maybe you were just in the right place at the right time, or maybe there's something about you that attracted her. It's definitely strange and we don't know all the answers. We don't even know the questions. But whatever it is, it's real or it wouldn't keep happening. I don't think you should look at it as something bad. We just need to figure out some stuff."

"Like what?"

"Well, let's start with what the power is. We need to investigate it." Connor looked at Sarah and Molly. "Right?"

"Absolutely," Sarah said. "Liam, we'll get to the bottom of it."

"Okay, I'm willing to try to figure out what's going on. But you guys can't tell anyone

about this. I don't want to be the school dork .
. . well, any more than I already am."

"Not a word," Connor said.

"I won't say anything to anybody," Sarah
said. "And you're not a dork. We're maybe
just a little different than everyone else. I
think that's a good thing."

"Thanks, Sarah." Liam looked at Molly.
"You can't tell Mom or Dad."

"You already told Dad."

"I know, but he's so busy he's probably
already forgotten about it. I won't bring it up
again."

"Yeah, you're right. Okay. I won't tell
anyone, either. Especially not Mom or Dad."

"All right. Where do we start?" Liam asked.

"How about with that old record," Sarah
suggested.

"That's a great idea," Connor exclaimed and
hurried out of the room.

Liam wasn't so sure. The very last thing he
wanted to do was see the girl in the tie-dye
shirt again.

* 75 *

***

Connor returned with the album. "So, what do we do?"

"I'm not sure."

"Just hand it to him and see what happens," Molly said.

"No. You should do exactly what you did the first time," Sarah said.

"I'll put the same song on to make it as close as possible to before."

As the music began, Liam lay down on the floor and Connor held out the record. Liam eyed it cautiously. He didn't want to touch it, but if there was a chance they could figure out why it was happening, and how to make it go away, then he had to try. He reached for the album and closed his eyes.

Instantly, she was there, but this time she was looking right at him. Her eyes were huge, brown orbs, shiny with tears. Her skin had turned from splotchy to bright red as if she'd been crying for hours. He felt waves of emotions coming from her—sadness, worry, joy, desperation, and fear . . . deep, in-the-gut terror. She watched him watching her.

Liam's skin crawled as if tiny ants skittered down the back of his neck. His breath caught and tears welled in his eyes. Quickly, he pushed the album away and sat up.

"Guys, this has officially become the weirdest thing . . . ever."

"Did you see her?" Sarah asked.

"Oh yeah. But that's not all. I could *feel* her. And . . ." *Should I tell them the rest of it? Will they believe it?* He decided to go for it. "She looked straight at me. She knows I can see her."

# CHAPTER SIX

**T**hey heard the garage door opening. By the time Connor's parents walked in, they were all sitting in the living room as if nothing had happened.

"Hey," Mr. Harrison said, his bushy brows arched in surprise. "What are you all up to?"

"Just listening to some records." Connor held up the *Eat a Peach* album cover.

"Did you find any treasures at the yard sales?" Connor's mom asked.

Neither of Connor's parents were very tall, but Connor's mother, Katie, was at least a head shorter than her husband. To Liam, she looked like a bottle brush—very slender with a thick mop of curly, lion's-mane hair.

"Not really," Molly said.

"Mostly just old junk," Liam added.

"I think this annual sale thing has been going on so long that people are selling what they bought at a neighbor's house the year before," Mrs. Harrison said. "Do you kids want to stay for lunch?"

"No thanks," Liam said. "Me and Molly better get home to see if our mom needs help cleaning up."

"Me too," Sarah said.

They started for the door, then Sarah turned back. "Hey, Connor. Don't forget to ask your folks about going to Liam's house tonight."

"Uh . . ."

"We're going to get a head start on that school project, remember?"

"Oh yeah." He got the hint. "Is it okay if I go over?"

Mrs. Harrison glanced at her husband and an odd look passed between them.

"Sure," Katie said. "Getting a jump on a school project is always good."

Liam knew his friends were trying to help, but he wasn't sure if he was ready to see the girl again. *What if she tries to talk to me this time?* A shiver of dread ran down his spine.

*\*\**

Liam and Molly spent the afternoon cleaning up after the garage sale. It always took longer than expected because of their mom's "nothing comes back into the house" rule. This meant that anything that wasn't sold would either be thrown away or donated.

Liam was starving as he grabbed his dinner plate and joined Molly and his mom on the back patio. His mom was telling a funny story about an elderly man buying some of the old books. He would lift one out of the box, squint at the cover, then hold it up.

"I must've read him every title and most of the blurbs on the back." She shook her head. "At least he bought a lot of them. He said that he and his wife liked to read romance novels to each other."

They were laughing when the side gate opened and Connor and Sarah walked in.

"Hello, MacLeod family!" Connor said as he sauntered up to the table and took a seat. "Are you all rich from selling your valuables?"

"I got thirty dollars for my old fish tank," Molly replied.

"Not bad."

"I made a whopping thirteen dollars," Liam said as he shoved the last bite of sandwich into his mouth.

"Huh, guess your junk was not as good as Molly's junk."

"How are your moms doing, Sarah? Heather usually has a lot of great items for the sale," Liam's mom said.

"She did. I'm not exactly sure where she hides it all. The stuff seems to come out of the woodwork on sale day. They sold a lot of it, so that's good."

"Hey, Liam, are you ready to get started on our project?" Connor asked.

"Project? I didn't know about that. What is it?" Michelle asked.

"What's what?" Connor said. Obviously buying time while he thought.

"What is the project?"

Liam could see Connor stumbling and sprang into the conversation. "It's about things you can't explain."

Liam's mom looked at them, puzzled.

"Yeah. We have to do a paper about an unexplainable event. Like supernatural stuff. You know, ghosts or zombies. Stuff like that."

"That sounds like an odd topic for a school project."

"Our teacher said she wants us to think 'outside of the box.'" Sarah made air quotes.

"Okay." Liam's mom shook her head. "You can go work on it once Liam finishes dinner and cleans up."

Quickly, Liam ate the rest of his chips and took his plate into the kitchen. The three were heading up the steps to his room when he heard Molly come into the house.

"I'm going with them," she said, rinsing her plate.

"No. You should let them do their work, honey."

From the upstairs hallway, Liam leaned over the railing. "It's okay, Mom. She can come. She knows a lot about zombies."

Michelle looked at him in amazement. "Well . . . okay."

"Thanks, Liam," Molly whispered as she joined him.

"No problem. We're a team, and you *do* know about zombies."

\*\*\*

"What did you mean earlier when you said she saw you, too?" Sarah asked as soon as they were in Liam's room with the door shut.

"When the visions first started, I could only see her profile. When it happened in orchestra practice, I thought she had turned slightly. This time, there was no doubt. She looked right at me."

"Oh man, that's creepy." Connor rubbed his arms as if the temperature in the room had suddenly dropped.

"Tell me about it," Liam said. "It's as if she wants something from me."

"We really need to get this figured out," Sarah said.

"Yeah, before Mr. Walsh tells my folks I can't play my bass. Mom's been bugging me to do the demo tape for the honors program and I won't be able to put her off much longer."

"So, where do we start?" Connor asked.

Liam turned on his computer. "I looked up some stuff the first night but didn't get very far."

Connor and Sarah read over Liam's shoulder.

"This is good, but you need to get more specific. Remember that old movie with the kid who saw dead people?" Connor asked.

"You mean *Sixth Sense*," Molly said. "That was so cool."

"Yeah. That's the one. So, the kid had ESP but could only use it to see dead people. There must be different kinds of ESP. Let's figure out what kind you have."

"What if you put in something like 'ESP by touch'?" Sarah suggested.

Liam typed it in and hit enter. Connor read the Wikipedia entry out loud:

Psychometry also known as token-object reading, or psychoscopy, is a form of extra-sensory perception characterized by the claimed ability to make relevant associations from an object of unknown history by making physical contact with that object. Supporters assert that an object may have an energy field that transfers knowledge regarding that object's history.

Psychometry is commonly offered at psychic fairs as a type of psychic reading. At New Age events psychometry has claimed to help visitors "meet the dearly departed"

Although the majority of police departments polled do not use psychics and do not consider them credible or useful on cases, some authors write that psychometry and psychic detectives were used by law enforcement agencies on specific cases.

"Ability to make relevant associations from an object of unknown history by making physical contact with that object," Liam read out loud. "That sounds about right. I'm not sure about all of the dearly departed stuff or solving crimes, though. What do you guys think?"

Connor flopped down on the bed. "That would be pretty cool if you could solve crimes."

"Maybe we need to solve the case of the girl in the blue tie-dye shirt." Molly sat up. "Figure out why she's bugging you."

"Do you think the girl's in trouble?" Connor asked.

"I don't know," Liam said. "Maybe. She's definitely afraid of something and upset."

"How do you know she's afraid?"

"I can feel it. Her fear."

"Maybe she was murdered and it's her ghost? Maybe Greg Ortman butchered her and buried her in this backyard?"

"Molly, where do you get this stuff?"

"I don't know. Mostly the British murder shows that Mom watches." She grinned at Liam.

"Well, I doubt that she was murdered, but there is something going on." Liam turned back to the computer and studied the results. "I just wish there was someone or someplace we could go to get better information. All the other results are just weird sites and stupid ads for psychic stuff."

"Why don't you look for a place around here?" Connor suggested.

Liam typed in *ESP* and added *Ozark* but only got hotels and a management company.

"Try 'mystics in Ozark,'" Sarah said.

"Yeah, right." Liam shot her a disgusted look, insulted at the idea of being called a mystic.

"Just saying it's worth a try."

Liam sighed and typed it in. The first thing that came up was an entry for a store called Cora's Crystals.

"The categories say *Rock Shops, Jewelry Designers, Gift Shops,* and *Mystical Products & Services.* It's not too far away from here—the corner of Main and Church."

"I know that place. It's over by the library. There's a cool mural on the outside. I've never been in there, though," Connor said.

"Does the shop have a website?" Sarah asked.

"Nope, just the phone number and address."

"Do you think the owner would know what psychometry is and how to make it go away?" Liam asked.

"Don't know, but it's worth a try. Right?"

Liam looked at the Google listing again. *Is this a place where I can find out more? Do I really have ESP or something like that?* The thought made him feel a little sick. If it turned out he was psychic and couldn't make it go away, then his whole life would change forever. He looked at the others. They were determined to help him understand what was happening. If they were brave enough, he was too.

"It looks like we're going on a field trip."

# CHAPTER SEVEN

**B**ells slung from the knob jangled when Liam opened the door to Cora's Crystals.

The shop was in an old Victorian-style house, and they walked into what must've once been the parlor. The first thing Liam noticed was the huge stone in the corner of the room. It had to be at least five feet tall, long and skinny with a domed top. The inside was hollow, as if carved out by nature, and glistened with sparkling, purple, multi-sided points that jutted toward the center.

"Wow! Look at that."

He walked over to the stone and studied the sharp purple facets that filled the interior. The display card tacked to the wall beside the stone said: *Amethyst geode. Origin—Brazil.*

*Quality—Very good. Strengthens your spiritual connection. Purifies your energetic body and supports release of old patterns, habits and addictions.* Liam wasn't sure what any of that meant, but he thought the stone was awesome. Gently, he placed a palm on the rough outer surface, and a jolt of something like electricity stabbed into his hand.

"Yow!" He jumped back.

"What's wrong with you? Did you get something?" Connor asked.

"No. A little jumpy, I guess." Liam turned away from the crystal, rubbing his hand on his thigh. Shelves covered in crystals and rocks were everywhere.

Molly was already digging through some of the bins as if she couldn't keep her hands off the stones. "Oh my gosh." She looked at him and grinned. "It's too bad Sarah had to work with her mom today. She would love this place. These are so cool. Look at this one." She held out a smooth, oblong piece that was lined with different shades of green.

Liam was reluctant to touch another stone. His hand still tingled from the last one, and he wondered if this was going to happen to him all the time now. Connor might think having a special ability was really cool, but Liam wasn't so sure.

He moved down the row of shelves, looking at the peculiar items on display. Besides the shelf of rocks that Molly was drooling over, there were at least eight others, all holding stones of incredible color and form. Tiny bottles lined one wall and colorful flags in different sizes hung from the ceiling. There was also a shelf holding only statues of the Buddha. Metal ones, wooden, glass, hand-painted, large and small. Beside the shelf sat a stuffed Buddha with a sign on his protruding belly that said, *Push here.* When Liam did, a deep sound of "Om" echoed through the shop.

"Look at this." Molly held up a small stone that looked like a miniature version of the big one in the corner. "I love this. Next time we come here, I'm bringing my allowance money."

Just then, a woman walked out of the back room and set a large box on the counter.

"Well, hello there." She looked calmly from Molly to Connor. "I didn't realize it was already Wednesday."

*What the heck does that mean?* Liam squirmed when her gaze settled on him with surprising intensity.

She was tall and thin with silver hair pulled back in a long braid. Beaded earrings hung from her ears and copper-colored bracelets jangled on her arm. The eyes that held his were a deep, clear blue.

She turned away and smiled at Molly, gesturing to the stone in her hand. "That is one of my favorites. It's a small amethyst geode."

"Oh, I . . . uh . . ." Molly gingerly set the stone back on the glass shelf.

"No worries, dear. They are meant to be handled. Each one has a special vibration that can be helpful to you."

The woman picked up another stone. This one was light blue with bits of tan striping. "For instance, this is turquoise. Its vibration helps with balance."

"You mean, so you don't fall over?" Connor asked.

"No, not that kind of balance." The woman laughed gently. "The kind of balance that keeps your mind, body and spirit all in harmony."

"How does it work?" Molly asked.

"Well, that question is a bit complicated to answer, especially without boring you kids in a big hurry. Let's just say that each stone comes out of the earth bearing a unique property—what you might think of as a vibration. When you hold it close, the essence of the crystal mixes with you and sets up a kind of echo that helps your body with healing, calming, clearing the mind, all sorts of things."

"She sounds just like Yoda," Connor whispered to Liam.

"Thank you, young man. Yoda is one of my heroes." She walked to one of the shelves and selected a smooth stone in a deep burgundy color. "See what you think of this one." She dropped it in Connor's hand and turned her gaze back to Liam. "My name is Cora, by the way."

"I'm Liam. This is my sister, Molly, and my friend Connor."

"It is very nice to meet you all. What brings you to my little shop? Are you just looking around, or is there something I can help you with?"

Liam exchanged glances with the others. They'd planned what to say, but it was Liam's job to make it sound like the truth.

"Uh, well . . . we have this paper we're working on for school, and we thought maybe you could help answer some questions."

"Sure. What kind of questions?"

"The paper is about things that are hard to explain. Stuff that you can't prove or easily understand."

"Are you talking about psychic ability, that sort of thing?"

"Yes, exactly. So, one of the topics for this paper is a guy who touches things and sees stuff that actually isn't there. We want to know if that can really happen and how it would work."

"I see. That's an interesting subject for a school paper. What made you think of it?"

Liam felt a surge of panic at Cora's unexpected question. He stared at her, racking his brain.

"Actually, I thought of it." Molly came to his rescue. "I heard Liam talking to our dad about the paper and told him about a show I saw on PBS. It was all about psychic stuff. Really cool."

"Ah, I see. Well, grab those two copper L-shaped things hanging on the wall behind you. Bring them over along with the amethyst geode."

Once Molly set the odd-looking pair of metal holders and the stone on the wooden countertop, Cora said, "I'm sure you learned in your science classes that the activities of cells and tissue generate electrical current. This can be detected and measured on the surface of the skin." She looked around at the three and each nodded.

"Do you also know that any electrical current creates a magnetic field in the surrounding area?" When they nodded again, she smiled. "Good. This is the biomagnetic field, the energy field. It surrounds everything and can be measured and mapped. It has actually been suggested that diseases of the body can be detected in this energy field before any physical symptoms appear." She waved her hand. "But that's a topic for later. Right now, I want to show you the effects of the energy field. Come on outside."

They followed her through the back of the store and into a large yard surrounded by a high wooden fence. A huge oak tree stood in the center and, even though it was not quite spring, dozens of brightly colored flowers grew along the fence.

She pointed at Liam and Connor. "You two stay here. Molly, go stand about halfway between the tree and the fence."

Once Molly was in place, Cora handed the rods to Connor. "Hold these by the handles with the long ends pointed toward Molly. Try to keep them close to each other and as level as you can. Now, slowly walk toward her."

Connor did as she said, and when he got to within a few feet, the rods spread apart, suddenly pointing in right angles to Molly. "What the heck? I didn't do that. I was holding them really steady."

Cora took the rods. "I know you were. That's exactly what they are supposed to do." She handed the rods to Liam. "Here, give it a try."

As he walked slowly toward Molly, he could feel the rods begin to vibrate. When he was a few feet away, they separated just as they had for Connor.

* 99 *

"Let me try. Let me try!" Molly bounced.

They all took turns holding the rods and being the subject; then Cora said, "I want to show you one more thing."

She gave the shafts to Liam and walked out into the yard. "Okay, come toward me."

Liam took only three steps and the dowsing rods separated. "Hey, what happened? I'm not even close to you."

"Now, come toward me again."

He slowly walked toward her, and this time the rods didn't separate until he was within two feet of her.

"I don't get it. Why is it different?"

"Come with me and I'll tell you."

Rather than leading them back into the shop, Cora took them to a screened porch off the back of the house. She gestured to chairs scattered loosely in a circle around a table inset with small, square tiles of vibrant colors.

"Anyone want some iced tea?"

Molly jumped up. "I'll help you."

"No, no. You sit here and think about what you just experienced. I'll be right back."

Once she was gone, Liam looked at his friend and sister. "What do you guys think?"

"Those metal things are rigged in some way," Connor said, settling back into his chair. "I know I didn't make them move."

"Uh-uh." Molly shook her head. "I don't know exactly how it works, but it's real. I could feel it."

Liam remembered the tingling in his fingers when he touched the rods and the crystals. He didn't know what it meant yet or how it applied to the tie-dye shirt girl, but he'd definitely felt something. Slowly, he nodded. "Yeah, there was something."

Cora came back onto the porch carrying a tray loaded with glasses, a plate of cookies, and a pitcher of iced tea. She took a sip of her tea, then settled her sharp gaze on Liam. He busied himself snagging a cookie.

"Have you figured out how it works yet?" Cora asked. When Liam and Connor shook their heads, she turned to Molly. "How about you?"

"Um, sort of . . . I think. It has to do with electricity, right? They detect it in some way."

"Exactly. That's using your noodle in a good way. It's in a field surrounding your body. The copper things are dowsing rods and they can detect that energy."

"Like the force field around the *Millennium Falcon*. Right?" Connor asked.

"Yes, more or less."

"So, how come when I walked toward you I got two different responses?" Liam asked.

"Ah. That's the fun part," Cora said. "I know how to shift my energy field. Expand and contract it. The rods responded accordingly."

"Awesome," Molly said. "Can you teach me how to do that?"

"Sure, but not today." Cora selected a cookie for herself, took a bite and slowly chewed. "Liam, what you are asking about is a psychic gift called *psychometry*. It's the ability to read or sense the energy patterns attached to an object. The impressions can come in the form of images, sounds, smells, tastes—even emotions."

"Okay, but how?"

"Think about what you just experienced. Do you believe that you were detecting some kind of energy field?"

He thought back to his experience in the yard. It was as if his hands prickled right before the rods separated. He met Cora's eyes. "Yes, I do."

"Good. Now take that belief a step further. Think about that energy field, which surrounds everything, holding imprints about that person or object. It's really not such a stretch. We know that matter on a subatomic level exists essentially as vibration. When you handle an object, the vibration of your cells mingles with the vibration of its cells. This would be particularly true during a traumatic or meaningful event. Sort of like an energetic fingerprint that's left behind. There can be either a light impression or a strong one.

Someone with the gift of psychometry is simply able to decode the vibration and receive a sense of what's been left behind."

With a click of understanding, Liam got it. The emotions from the girl were trapped in the album cover, and for some weird reason he could feel it. The same with the old desk and the kids who were in the tornado.

"So, if a person senses another person from an object, does that mean they're communicating with them?"

"Hmm. Usually it's residual energy that's felt, not something interactive." Cora sipped her tea. "But that's definitely possible. When a person has this ability, touching an object sets up a kind of conduit. If that connection is to another person, then communication could happen. And there's always the possibility that someone with psychometric ability could also have another ability as well, like clairvoyance."

*Oh, that's just great! I might have two psychic abilities? I don't want to have any!*

"So, if somebody had this . . . er . . . gift, and they didn't want it, is there a way to make it go away?" Liam asked.

"Well, to me it seems that being able to read energy that most people can't would be an amazing gift. That person could probably help a lot of people, so why would they not want to use it?"

"Help people how?" Liam asked.

"I'm sure in many ways. I've heard of it being used by police departments to find missing people and to solve crimes."

"Are psychic people born that way?" Connor asked.

"Some are, and some become aware of their abilities through life experiences."

"What kind of experiences?" Molly asked, sitting forward in her chair.

"Well, usually by some sort of significant event. To the physical body or to the psyche. A blow to the head, especially on the left side, can trigger a psychic ability that has been buried. The right side, the creative side, compensates for any damage done to the left, which is the analytical side."

She glanced at Liam, and Liam could almost feel her eyes touching the spot on his left temple where the hair was growing back over his scar.

"And how does somebody get the ability in the first place?" Molly pressed.

"That's an easy one. It's passed down genetically, just like your beautiful blue eyes." Cora set her glass on the table and stood up. "Well, that's all the questions I have time for today. I need to get back to work. Restocking to do and a class tonight."

Liam, Molly, and Connor followed her back through the shop. At the front door, Liam turned.

"Can I ask you one more thing?"

"Of course, Liam. What is it?"

"If someone wanted to actually try to use psychometry or that other thing, how would they do it?"

"Well, the best way would be for the person to sit quietly. They should hold the item and take deep, calming breaths. Focus on bringing energy from the object into their awareness. If they paid attention to the impressions that came into their mind, they might find out useful information about the object. It would be more difficult to do if the person felt anxious or stressed."

"Thank you, Cora," Liam said. His head was throbbing from all the information. He wanted to get to some quiet place so that he could think about what she'd said.

"You're welcome. Come back anytime." She walked with them to the shop door and they stepped onto the front porch. "Liam, I hope that you do well on your paper. If you ever meet someone who has this ability, please tell him to stop by my shop. I'd like to meet him."

Liam shrugged but knew his cover was blown.

"Oh, one more thing." She handed each of them a stone. "These are for you. Next time you come in, you can tell me what your impressions are."

Liam's fingers curled around the sparkling, reddish-gold stone she laid in his palm. He'd learned a lot from Cora, and its pulsing didn't surprise him now. If the album was a channel to the tie-dye girl, maybe he could use it to talk to her. That idea was very disturbing, but it might be worth trying. He could find out why she was bugging him and ask her to go away.

# CHAPTER EIGHT

A statue of a Civil War soldier sat in the middle of the town square. It was surrounded by a frothing fountain and held a stern look on its face. It seemed to be staring down at the city hall building.

Liam pulled up to the concrete wall and got off his bike. He slouched onto the ledge and watched as Molly and Connor dismounted and propped their bikes alongside. When they joined him, he sighed.

"What do we do now?" Molly asked.

"I really don't know," Liam groaned. "But it sounds like I have this ability."

"Dude, you totally do. Psychometry and that clair-whatsit," Connor said. "You bashed your head on the rocks and *POW!* You're psychic. Kinda like that girl in *Christmas Vacation*. You know. She fell down a well and got cross-eyed. Then she got kicked in the head by a mule and her eyes went back to normal. Maybe if you smash your head again, it would go away?"

"Ha ha. Don't tempt me." Liam glowered. "At least I have a better idea of what's happening. I still don't know how to get rid of the girl and get my life back, though."

Connor jumped up and started walking atop the wall as if it were a tightrope. A few paces away from them, he pirouetted and started back. "There really is only one thing we can do."

"Oh yeah, what's that?" Liam squinted up into his friend's face.

"We have to find Greg Ortman. Find him, and that will lead us to the girl."

"I agree," Molly said.

"Are you both insane?" Liam jumped up.

"I'm not. How about you, Connor?"

"Nope."

*No way. Uh-uh. Not going to happen.* If they went on a search for Greg Ortman, somewhere along the way others would find out about his new "gifts." It was bad enough being the tallest kid in school and a nerdy musician, but Brandon and his buddies would start calling him a lot worse than "Lurch" if they found out he was psychic.

"You know, guys, all I really want to do is play music and not be noticed."

"Dude, if you get accepted to the honors program, you'll be performing at Carnegie Hall. You're gonna get noticed."

"Yeah, but that's different. I'll be with the rest of the orchestra."

He thought about the girl. *Did she actually look at me?* A chill went down his back when he thought about Cora saying that some people with his ability helped the police find missing people. *Is that what I need to do? Is she lost and wanting me to find her? Do I really have any other choice?*

"Okay, let's find Greg Ortman. But we need a plan, and we don't have a lot of information to go on."

"Just the name, Greg Ortman, and Google," Molly said. "Sarah can help us. She can research anything."

"That's as good a start as any," Connor said. "You could also try to get more information from the record."

"He's right," Molly said. "Cora said it was a gift. You might as well use it."

"Yeah. I was thinking of that, but . . ." His stomach shot to his knees. This was all too new. He didn't want to be frightened of this, but he really didn't know what the girl would do next. *Will she talk to me?* That upped the creepy factor considerably, but he didn't see any other way out. "Okay. I'll try my hardest but won't make any promises."

"Dude, I think you need to figure out how not to try hard," Connor said. "Based on what Cora said, it seems like you need to find a way to relax and just let it happen."

"Easier said than done."

"Maybe you should go back to Cora's and talk to her about it," Molly said.

"I think I'll try some stuff on my own first. Let's get home."

"Why don't you stop at my house first and pick up the record?" Connor asked. "You can take it with you."

*** 

After dinner, Liam went straight to his room. He sat in his desk chair and eyed the album sitting on the desk. *Okay. I can do this.* He took a deep breath and slid the album onto his lap. He tried to clear his mind, but his thoughts tumbled over each other and the girl didn't appear. *What the heck? She's usually in my face all the time. Where'd she go?* With a sigh, he put down the record and turned on his computer. *Maybe I can find a relaxation method online.*

After ten minutes of looking, he found a technique to try. He shifted around until he got comfortable in the chair and set the record in front of him. He took a few deep breaths, closed his eyes and started slowly counting backward from ten, imagining each number fading away into the distance.

Slowly, he set his hands on the record. The now-familiar vertigo sensation came over him and the image of the girl appeared. *Relax and breathe. She can't hurt you.* He focused on the image, the background. There she was, wearing the tie-dye T-shirt. She stood in front of a bed, sobbing. When she began to turn toward him, he held his breath. He wanted to toss the album away but steeled himself for what would come next.

When she faced him fully, tears flowing down her red-splotched cheeks, her hand rose toward him. He shivered in anticipation of her icy touch on his chest. Fear stuttered through him. He knew that some of it was his but that most came from her. When her lips moved, he tensed. *She's going to talk to me. This is too unbelievable.* He wanted to stop, longed for all of this to go away. He didn't want to know what she wanted. He couldn't help her. He was just a kid with his own problems. The word *Help* formed on her lips and screamed into his head. A dagger of pain staggered him. He dropped the album and rolled onto the bed, clutching his temples. As the vision of the girl faded and the throbbing eased, a new image arose—a building with weathered siding hanging askew and jagged shards of glass where windows had been. Knowing it was important, Liam tried to hold onto the vision, but it vanished with a pop. While the image was still fresh in his mind, Liam sketched it onto a piece of notebook paper and shoved it into his backpack.

As he drifted off to sleep, he thought about what he'd done. *Maybe this gift isn't so scary after all.* The addition of the building was a clue. He just didn't know where it fit into the puzzle . . . yet.

***

The next day, Liam sat at the lunch table and unpacked his paper bag. PB&J with pretzels, yogurt and a banana, same as every day. Connor came up and slapped his tray down.

"Man, you don't know what you're missing. The hamburgers here are the best."

"Yeah, right," Liam said, then told Connor about seeing the weathered building. "It looked like an old factory. I know it's important, but I don't know what it means."

"I've been thinking about Greg Ortman." Sarah plunked her retro Partridge Family lunch box and beaded, purple bag down on the table and slid onto the bench next to them. "We need to find him. He should be easy enough to narrow down online. It's an unusual name, and I can't imagine there are that many Greg Ortmans in the world."

"Yeah, we already figured that out," Connor garbled around the bite of burger in his mouth.

"That's really gross, Connor." He grinned at her and she shook her head. "So, where'd you get the record?"

"My uncle bought it at a record shop in Kenosha."

She put her elbows on the table, propped her head on her hand and gazed into the distance. Liam recognized the look.

Connor said, "But–"

"Shhhh. She's thinking."

"You know," Sara finally said, "if we could find out where the shop gets their records, that would help. They may get them from local people, and that would narrow the search to Kenosha and towns close by. Then, when we get a small enough list, we can just start making calls."

"You're a genius. That's a great idea," Liam said.

"Hold it." Connor shook his head. "I don't think we should be calling people about the record."

"Why not?"

"Yeah, why not?" Liam asked. "It was your idea to find him."

Connor just stared at him as if he should already know the answer. Finally, he leaned forward and whispered, "Well, how about the fact that you don't know who this Greg Ortman is? Cora said that sometimes people with your gift help the police. The girl is crying, right? Maybe something happened to her? Maybe he killed her?"

"Huh. Now that I think about it, you may have a point," Sarah said.

"What? You don't really think Greg Ortman killed the girl, do you?" Liam asked her.

"No, of course not. But we should try to find out as much as we can before you talk to him."

"Told you," Connor said, looking at Liam.

Liam ignored him and focused on Sarah.

"I can totally help you guys," Sarah said. "We can find him, I know it. And once we do, we can figure out what our next steps should be."

"Find who, kiddies?"

Liam whirled around. Kaylee and Dylan sat on the table behind them and Brandon leered from beside. He snatched Connor's burger from the plate, took a giant bite and dropped the rest on the floor.

"Hey." Connor lunged to his feet. "That was my lunch."

"Really? I thought it was some turd you dropped. Tasted like it."

"You're disgusting," Sarah said. She shoved her sandwich back into her lunch box.

Brandon leaned across the table, his face close to hers. "Oh yeah? Well, you're stupid."

Liam thrust to his feet. He towered over the shorter kid but didn't feel bigger . . . stronger.

"Leave us alone," he said, but even to his own ears, his voice sounded lame.

"Yeah," Connor said. "Why don't you just crawl back under your rock?"

Kaylee and Dylan moved to flank their friend.

Brandon took a step closer to Liam. Liam could smell the kid's sour sweat and it made him slightly nauseous.

"Make me, Lurch." He shoved Liam backward into the table.

"Stop it," Sarah cried and swung her lunch box into Brandon's stomach.

The bully chuffed out a breath and grabbed his abdomen.

"What's going on here?" The lunchroom monitor appeared behind Connor.

"Nothing, Ms. Baker." Dylan swung Brandon around and the three disappeared through the double doors leading to the hallway.

"Are you kids okay?"

Liam looked at his friends. "Yes, we're fine." But he knew they weren't, and sooner or later they would have to deal with Brandon and the other two.

*** 

When Liam and Molly got to the library, Connor and Sarah were already there sitting at a computer. Liam was surprised and a little annoyed to see David, Sarah's younger brother, with them. He'd always thought the kid was a little strange because he only dressed in black and hardly ever talked. Most of the time, he wore headphones and bobbed his head to music the rest of the world couldn't hear.

"Hey, guys," Liam said as he took off his backpack. "Uh, what are you doing?"

Sarah glanced over her shoulder. "Duh. What do you think?"

Liam flicked his eyes toward David and raised his eyebrows.

"Oh. No worries. He knows everything and has taken a solemn oath to not tell. Right, Connor?"

"Yup. I was the witness, so we're good."

Liam groaned. This was getting way out of hand. At this rate everyone would know his secret by next week.

Sarah typed and clicked through web pages so fast that Liam had a hard time keeping up.

Finally, she looked at him, her eyes huge behind giant, bedazzled cat-eye glasses.

"Look at this. There are four Greg Ortmans in our general area and one of them works at the Kenosha Fire Department. It says his birthday is in 1972. When was the record made?"

"Same year," Connor said.

"It doesn't seem like this would be the right guy, then. The room in the vision looked Seventies-ish. You know, beanbags, posters on the wall, shag rug," Liam said.

"And the girl's wearing a tie-dye shirt," Connor added.

"Okay." Sarah turned back to the computer. "I can't find any information about two of them and the last one is even younger than the man in Kenosha."

"Well, crud," Molly said. "I guess we hit a dead end."

"Why don't you go down to Kenosha? You can find that guy and see if it really is a dead end."

Surprised, Liam looked at David, who hadn't said a word until then.

"What do you mean?" Connor said.

"Kenosha's only thirty minutes away. Go to the record store."

"That's brilliant," Connor said. "We can ask the people at the store where they get their records. Heck, they may even know Greg Ortman."

"If he works in Kenosha, he must live there, too. Does the computer show his address?" Molly asked.

"No, I can't get that kind of information without paying for a search service," Sarah said.

"I don't know, guys. It seems like a wild goose chase," Liam said.

"It may be, but do you have a better idea?" Connor asked.

Liam shook his head. "No, and I need to get this figured out soon."

"How would we get there?" Molly asked.

"Dad," Liam said. "We're at his house this weekend. He would take us if we came up with a good enough reason."

"Uh, Liam, that's a terrible idea. He's not going to just take us to Kenosha. Besides, we're supposed to work on the cabin this weekend, remember? He would think it was weird if we didn't want to help."

She was right. There was no way his plan would work. "Okay, so we'll ride our bikes. We can tell him we'd rather do the river trail than go to the lake property. We can all go and tell him it's for a school project or something."

"Liam," Sarah said, "it's thirty-five miles to Kenosha. Just there and back on a bike would be about five hours. There wouldn't be any time left over to find the guy."

"Well, I want to go," Connor said. "My folks are doing a juice cleanse this weekend and that's really gross. No way am I sticking around the house."

"What's a juice cleanse?" Molly asked.

"Trust me, you don't want to know."

"How about the bus?" Liam asked. "We could ride our bikes to the town square and then catch the bus from there to Kenosha. If we leave early enough, that should give us plenty of time."

"That might work." Sara leaned forward, squinting at the screen as her fingers tapped over the keyboard. "There's a bus that leaves here at 7:30 AM. It has a bunch of stops along the way but eventually gets to Kenosha at 8:45 AM. There's a stop near the Kenosha town square. That'd be pretty close to the record shop. The next bus isn't until 11:30. That wouldn't give us enough time."

"7:30 in the morning? How would we explain that to Dad?" Molly asked.

Liam lowered his head. He hadn't thought about how to elude his parents and really didn't want to do it now. "I have no idea."

"Maybe we could sneak out before Dad and Jennifer wake up," Molly said.

"Nah, that would never work. Even if we got out, we'd never be back before everyone was up."

They were so close, but he just couldn't figure out a way to . . . When the solution popped into his brain, he smiled.

"Wait. I've got it. Connor, tell your folks you want to spend the night at our place. Molly, we'll tell Dad we're staying at Connor's. Sarah, you'll need to figure out what to say to your moms."

"Uh, okay, but . . . where're we really going to stay?"

"We're spending the night at the Orpheum. The theatre's been abandoned forever. Nobody would ever know we're there."

There was a collective gasp, then everyone began talking at once.

When the librarian shushed them, Liam leaned in. "We gotta do this and soon. Full-on for Friday?"

The others nodded and the girl swirled across his vision. He didn't even question the weirdness of it, just took it as a sign that he was on the right track.

"We'll have to figure out a way to get in without being seen," Connor said.

"Yeah. We'll create the plan as we go. Connor, talk to your parents, and we'll do the same. Bring a blanket and some food to school and we'll go from there to the Orpheum."

"What about you, Sarah? What're you going to say to your moms?"

Sarah shrugged. "Don't know yet, but I'll think of something."

"So, we're doin' this."

Connor stuck his hand out in the middle of the group.

"What are you doing?"

"I just thought we should break." He glanced around at the blank faces. "You know, like a football team huddle. Maybe do a cheer or something." They all just shook their heads and walked off.

"You guys are just going to leave me hanging?"

"Yep," Liam said, not looking back.

"I still think we should come up with a cheer," Connor said and reluctantly followed his friends.

# CHAPTER NINE

**L**iam slid his bass into the back and climbed into his dad's jeep. "How was practice?" Lloyd asked.

"Not too bad," Liam lied. There was no way he could tell his dad that he'd been unable to play again because the vision of the girl had been in his face. "We're still having trouble with 'Don't Fear the Reaper.' Tina just can't get the timing right. We need more practice on it. But I'm really pumped about playing 'Closer to the Heart.'"

"Yeah," Lloyd said. "Rush is a cool band. Remember when we went to Kenosha last year to see them? We should do that again sometime. I love the concert venue there."

"Sure, Dad. That would be fun." The mention of Kenosha made Liam's heart skip a beat. *No, no, no. Not this weekend. Please don't say this weekend.* "Hey, Dad? Would it be okay if I slept over at Connor's on Friday?"

His dad shot him a glance and then looked back at the road. "Well . . . I guess so. You don't want to help out at the lake? We're starting to clear the area down on the point. Open up the view some."

"Yeah, that sounds cool, but Connor and I decided to enter the school talent contest and want to practice the song we picked."

"Talent contest? I haven't heard about that. When is it?"

*Oh man, this just keeps getting worse.* He didn't even know if there really was a contest. "Uh, it's, er . . . well, I'm not exactly sure. Connor told me about it. I'll get more details from him on Friday. Molly said she might come too. She wants to play with the puppies."

Lloyd didn't say anything. As the silence lengthened, Liam became sure that his dad was suspicious about the change of plans.

"Something going on you want to tell me about?" Lloyd asked.

"What? No. Just . . . It's kind of important."

Liam's dad stared at him a moment and then, thankfully, the light changed. "Okay. I don't see why not. We'll miss your help at the lake, though."

"I know, Dad. I'll help next time, promise."

They pulled up in front of Liam's mom's house and he started to get out. His dad laid a hand on his arm. "You know you can tell me anything, right?"

"Sure, Dad." Liam smiled. "I'll see you on Saturday."

Liam stood next to his bass case and watched his dad drive away. He hated lying to his parents. It wasn't something that he did very often and he felt awful. But he just couldn't see any other way. His dad would never let him seek out Greg Ortman, even if he did believe the bizarre things that were going on.

***

During lunch on Friday, Liam relayed the conversation with his dad to Connor and Sarah. "I'm not sure if he believed me or not. I checked, though, and there really is a talent contest, so if he asks the school, I'm in the clear."

"Maybe we should enter. We could do 'Fly by Night,' or how about 'Working Man'?" Connor asked.

"Yeah, maybe, but right now we need to focus on finding Greg Ortman . . . and getting into the Orpheum.

"What'd you tell your moms about tonight, Sarah?"

"That we're staying with Bianca. She has a younger brother that's friends with David. They didn't ask too many questions. I think they were happy to get some time to themselves."

"You didn't tell Bianca what's going on, did you?" Connor looked worried.

"Of course not. Jeez. I'm not an idiot."

"I didn't mean . . ."

"I know. It's okay. I think we're all a little nervous about tonight . . . and tomorrow."

"That's for sure," Connor said. "If we get caught, we're dead."

"A bit melodramatic, don't you think?" Sarah scoffed.

"Actually, no." Liam frowned. "For sure, me and Molly would be grounded until . . . forever. You know, you guys don't have to risk it if you don't want to. I would understand." His stomach sank at the thought of doing this by himself, but he didn't have a choice. Until he figured out what was happening with the girl and got her out of his life, the future he had planned was lost.

"Are you kiddin', dude? No way I'm letting you have all the fun." Connor clapped him on the back.

"He's right," Sarah said. "We're in this to the end."

"So, I guess we're really on for tonight, then. I stuffed some blankets in my backpack and Molly said she was going to bring food. She's meeting us at the bike racks after school."

"David, too," Sarah added.

"Do you realize what today is?" Connor asked.

Liam glanced at Sarah, who shook her head. "No, what?"

"It's the first 'First Friday' of the year. The square will be packed with people."

"Uh-oh. That could be a problem," Liam said.

"I don't think so. All the noise and people will give us perfect cover. You know, in case we make noise breaking in or something."

"We are *not* going to break in," Sarah said. "We're just going to see if any of the doors or windows are unlocked and go in if we find a way."

"Yeah, but what if our folks decide to go to the First Friday? Then what?"

"My folks won't be there. Juice cleanse, remember? Your dad is focused on the new cabin, and you said your mom had choir practice. Miss Heather and Miss Rachel hate big crowds. We'll be just fine."

"Yeah, I guess you're right." Liam rubbed sweaty palms on his pants legs. "There's just a lot at stake here."

"I know, but it's also very cool."

"Yeah, it is," Sarah agreed. "A night in the Orpheum. Wow! I've always wanted to tour that place."

"Well, I meant searching for Greg Ortman, but that too. We're a team . . . kind of like a club." Connor grinned. "Hey, we need a name."

"Connor, try to stay focused, will you?" Sarah rapped him on the forehead. "Greg Ortman. Girl. Weird psychic power. Remember."

"Yeah, yeah. And I don't think the fact that there's a Greg Ortman in Kenosha is a coincidence."

"I agree," Liam said. "I just hope we can figure out how to find him."

"Dude, you do realize that the Orpheum is probably full of old stuff. Anything you touch could send you into something far-out wild."

"Yeah, I thought about that. But it's a great place to hole up for the night, and we have to get to Kenosha. If anything happens, I'll just have to deal with it."

\*\*\*

Liam led them around a loudly beeping truck maneuvering into position to unload porta potties. He caught the aroma of french fries, onion rings, burgers, Mexican food, and Connor's favorite, mini-donuts. Hungry workers were already lined up for a meal. He stopped at the bike rack near the statue.

"Let's park here and work our way around to the Orpheum. Maybe we should split up.

That way it's not quite so obvious in case anyone sees us."

Connor stood by his bike, studying Sarah's and then David's. "This isn't going to work."

"What are you talking about?" Sarah swung around. "Of course it is. We have it all planned out."

"Not Kenosha, the bikes. We can't leave them here."

"Why not? I park my bike here all the time," Sarah said.

"Exactly. That's the problem. Everyone in town knows your bike. It may be the only rainbow-colored vintage Schwinn on the planet. And David's black BMX is too awesome to overlook."

Sarah looked at the bikes and sighed. "You're right. Once it gets late, they'll stand out. Someone is bound to see them and ask questions. What should we do?"

"We'll bring them with us and either take them into the Orpheum or hide them somewhere," Liam said.

"Come on, David," Molly said. "Let's go this way." They started across the street, pushing their bikes.

"Maybe we should get some food," Connor suggested. "You know. Just to fuel up for the night."

Sarah thumped him on the back. "Focus."

Liam shrugged. Food sounded good to him too, but she was right. They were on a mission and needed to concentrate.

They followed Sarah, trying to act as if they had no particular place to go, which Liam thought made them look even more obvious. Movement across the park caught his eye.

"Oh no! It's Brandon."

"What? Where?" Sarah scanned the street.

Connor followed Liam's gaze. "Over by the burger truck. He's in line."

"We've got to get out of here before he sees us," Liam said.

They ducked down an alley and circled around to the back of the Orpheum. Molly and

David's bikes were propped against a tree, but they were nowhere in sight.

"Molly," Liam hissed. She popped up from behind a row of shrubs and out-of-control weeds along the wall.

"We tried all of the windows here. They're locked."

"Well, no offense, but I'm going to try them again," Connor said and worked his way behind the shrubs.

They could hear him scrabbling around until he finally emerged from the other end, brushing leaves off his T-shirt and pulling twigs out of his long hair. "Those bushes are a great place to hide our bikes."

"Any luck with the windows?" Liam asked.

"No go." Connor shook his head. "I tried to look in, but it's really dark in there and the glass is dirty. We may have to break one."

"Uh-uh," Sarah said. "We're not breaking anything. If we can find an unlocked door or window, we'll go in, but otherwise . . . NO!"

"She's right. We would get into so much trouble if we got caught. Getting kicked out of orchestra would be the least of my problems. Let's try the other sides of the building. It's a little riskier, but worth a shot. Somebody needs to keep a lookout."

"I'll do it," Molly said. "If anybody gets nosy I'll do a bird call. Owl or crow?"

"Owl," Liam said, and she set off for the front of the building.

"Owl call?" Connor looked at Liam and grinned.

"Yeah. She watched a National Geographic show on bird calls a couple of years ago. She's actually pretty good."

Once she was gone, Liam pointed to Sarah and David. "You guys go check that side, me and Connor will check the other. Meet us back here when you're done."

There was a line of ground windows tucked behind shrubs, just like at the rear. Liam and Connor checked each one, but they were all locked. Liam wanted to growl in frustration.

The image of the girl in the blue tie-dye shirt floated up and his gut rolled.

"If we can't find a secret place to stay tonight, the entire plan will be blown," Liam said as they returned to the back of the building.

"I know. We have to figure something out."

"Find anything?" Liam asked Sarah when they came around the corner.

"There's a door on that side and we tried that too, but nothing."

"What the heck are we going to do?" Liam ran a hand through his hair, tempted to tug on it in frustration.

"Maybe we need to think of somewhere else to stay?" Connor suggested.

"Guys," David said.

"Yeah, but where? We can't camp because I'd have to ask to borrow gear from my dad and that'd mean a whole new set of lies."

"Uh, yoo-hoo. Guys."

"What?" Liam snapped at David.

The boy pointed and Liam looked up. Hidden behind the branches of a giant oak tree was a fire escape ladder.

Sarah gasped. "There's a window and a door. Maybe one of them is unlocked?"

Liam was the tallest, but no matter how high he stretched, he couldn't reach the lower rung. He tried jumping but still couldn't grasp it. "We need a ladder or something."

"No, we don't," Connor said. "Liam, stand here. Sarah, you're the next tallest. Climb onto Liam's shoulders."

"What? I don't think so. What if he drops me?"

"He's right." Liam gestured her over. "This will work. I won't drop you. I promise."

Obviously doubtful, Sarah inched toward him.

"Okay, Liam, squat down. Sarah, I'll help you get on."

With a few false starts and one near-drop, Sarah finally settled onto Liam's shoulders. It was a little uncomfortable, but once he had her balanced, it was okay.

"Can you reach it?" Connor asked.

"Almost. I need another inch or so."

Liam stood taller.

"Almost there. Just a little more. Liam, stand on your tiptoes."

Liam did and her weight eased when she grabbed the bottom rung of the fire escape.

"Got it. Now what?"

"Pull," Connor said.

She gave the metal a sharp tug. With a rusty screech, it careened down. The ladder struck Liam square in the chest, knocking him to his back. Sarah flew off and landed with a muffled scream. Connor ran over and eased her to a sitting position. She gasped for air and he pounded on her back.

"Stop it. Stop it, you idiot." She batted his hands away.

"Are you okay?" Liam sank down onto his knees beside her just as Molly rounded the corner.

"What's going on?"

"I'm fine. Got the breath knocked out of me for a sec, but it was worth it. Look." She pointed to the fire escape that was now within easy reach.

Suddenly, the metal groaned and started to rise. David flew toward it and leaped, barely catching the last rung. He hung, suspended for a moment, then the ladder settled to the ground with a clang.

"Jeez. Quiet," Connor said. "We don't want the whole town coming down on us."

"Good catch, though." Liam gestured up the ladder. "After you."

David led the way until they were all perched on a landing. Liam tried the doorknob, but it wouldn't budge. He shoved at it with his shoulder and then Connor joined him. Nothing. Liam stepped to the window and reached for the sill. He looked back at the group.

"Fingers crossed, 'cause if we can't get into one of these, I'm out of ideas." He grasped the base of the window and heaved. It didn't move. "Connor, give me a hand."

When they still couldn't get the window open, Liam looked at his friends. The discouragement he felt was engraved onto each face in pinched lips and flared nostrils.

"The little twerps came around here, I'm sure of it." An all-too-familiar voice floated up from below. "And I heard some kind of metallic sound."

Liam whirled and looked over the edge. Brandon, Kaylee, and Dylan stood right beneath them.

# CHAPTER TEN

Liam's hands clenched the rusty rail. His stomach dropped to the vicinity of his knees.

"Oh no," Molly whispered. "What do we do now?"

Liam mouthed, *Don't move.* If those guys saw them, they were dead. Still as stones, they watched as the three kids scanned the back of the building. *Don't look up, don't look up.* Liam repeated the chant silently, mentally pushing the bullies away. Slowly, they skulked along the back, kicking at the bushes where Connor had hidden the bikes.

As the minutes ticked by, sweat sprouted from Liam's brow and ran into his eyes. He sipped valuable air in shallow breaths. When the bullies finally disappeared around the corner of the building, he sagged against the rail. He and his friends had survived Brandon, but they still needed to get into the Orpheum or this would all be for nothing.

He heard a quiet tapping behind him. It seemed to be coming from inside the door. The tapping turned to rattling, then a deep groaning as metal rubbed against metal. Astonished, Liam turned to stare at the tightly locked door. As impossible as it seemed, it was shaking in its frame. Then, with a shower of dust and paint chips, it popped open.

"What the heck?" Connor gaped.

Sarah moved forward. "It was painted shut. You can see the dried globs."

"Yeah, but what opened it?" Molly asked.

Connor shrugged. "We must have set off some kind of chain reaction."

"Weird," Liam said. "But at least we're in." With a quick glance over the railing to make sure that Brandon and the others hadn't returned, he carefully stepped into the dark room. He stomped a few paces away and then came back. "The floor seems solid. Come on in."

The others sidled in and Liam gingerly pulled the door shut behind them.

*** 

The air was heavy with a sour musk. Particles of dust swam in the dim beams of light filtering through the dirty window. Liam heard the skittering of claws, and movement flashed in the corner.

"Rats," he whispered to no one in particular.

"Yuck." Sarah's voice trembled slightly and Liam understood why.

"This place is kinda spooky," Molly said, glancing over her shoulder like she expected something to jump out and grab her.

Through the murk and dangling cobwebs, Liam saw a desk, chair, and file cabinet in a corner of the room. "Must've been an office." The old boards creaked as he walked over. He reached out, then hesitated, studied the table.

Uncertainty prickled his scalp, but curiosity overcame it. No time like right now to start strengthening his gift. He placed his fingertips on the dust-laden wood, feeling the grain and pocks from decades of use.

"Getting anything?" Connor asked.

Liam shook his head. "Nothing. Maybe the visions have stopped," he said, surprised to find that he felt sad about that.

"Or there's nothing remarkable about that desk," Molly said. "Cora said that the energy transference was more likely if something traumatic happened, remember?"

Liam hoped Molly was right because it felt very weird to imagine life without his "gift" now. He wasn't sure when the idea had shifted into "normal," but it had. "Let's look for a good place to set up camp."

They followed Sarah down the hallway, batting at gossamer strands that blocked their way. She opened the door at the end.

"Oh cool," she said, walking over to a large window. She rubbed her palm across the dust-caked glass and peered through. "Look at this, guys."

It was barely light enough to see the theatre spread out below them with the crimson-curtain-draped stage at the front. Rows of long-empty seats were separated by a main aisle carpeted in dingy red.

"This is beautiful. Look at the woodwork on that ceiling! And the wainscoting. I bet there used to be a gigantic chandelier hanging above the seats."

"This must've been the control room." Liam glanced around the grimy interior and spotted pieces of ancient electronic equipment and spotlights shoved into the corners.

Connor walked to one of the lights and rubbed a hand over the dome. "Just think, this may have shone on some very famous dudes."

"What do you think about making this room our base for tonight?" Liam asked.

A door slammed somewhere in the building. They all jumped and Sarah pushed her fist against her chest. Liam held his breath. *Is someone else in the building?* When no other sound followed, he relaxed. "Must have been the wind."

"Are you sure?" Molly's eyes were wide. "It wasn't windy when we came in."

Liam shrugged. He stepped out into the hallway and looked both ways. Nothing lurked in the shadows except layers of dirt. "All clear."

Sarah drew a wide arc in the dust with the toe of her tennis shoe. "It would be nice if we could find a broom or something."

"Yeah," Molly said. "Let's go look around."

Liam led them into another room that had no outside windows and was inky black. He flicked on the light from his smartphone and played the beam into the darkness. The figure of a man loomed from the corner.

Liam choked and jumped back, bobbling the light so that the man's larger-than-life shadow bounced on the wall. "Somebody's here." He could barely gasp out the words. "We've gotta get out."

Stumbling, they turned to run. David stepped neatly out of the way, standing his ground. When he started laughing, they all stopped.

"I don't think he's going to hurt us," he said, walking over to the cardboard cutout.

"Oh, for gosh sakes," Sarah said, punching Liam in the shoulder. "You scared the life out of me."

"I wasn't scared," Connor said, inspecting the soldier standing alert, a rifle to his shoulder. "I'm bringing this bad boy back to the control room. He can stand guard tonight."

"Whatever," Sarah said. "But try to find something useful, too."

Boxes were crammed onto shelves in another corner and Connor inspected them, trying to read the faded labels. "Liam, bring your light over here."

"Anything good in there?" Sarah asked, sorting through some ragged blankets layered on a shelf.

"Nope," Connor said. "Looks like old receipts."

"These blankets will be good cushioning," Sarah said. "Let's pull them into the control room and then check out the rest of the place."

"Yeah, I want to go down to the stage," Connor said.

The light seeping in through the tiny, frosted-glass windows close to the ceiling was fading. With each step, the ragged aisle seemed to groan in protest of being neglected for so long. Shadows gathered in the corners of the cavernous room, and Liam thought he felt the eyes of hundreds of long-forgotten ghosts scuttling across his back as he walked down.

They pushed through ornately carved double doors and out into the lobby. A large wooden counter dominated the room. Dust was layered on top, and a sweep of Liam's hand revealed a stained but polished surface. At his touch, he smelled popcorn mingled with cigarette smoke. "This must've been the ticket counter and concession stand."

Connor sauntered up, put his elbows on the counter. "Five for *Gone with the Wind*, please." His affected Southern drawl was silly and they all laughed.

"What an amazing place," Molly said.

"It really is," Sarah said. "I just love old places. Imagine the stories it could tell."

Connor looked around the darkening lobby. "The light's fading and I want to get on that stage before it's too dark to see. Plus, we really shouldn't hang out here. Someone might spot us through the windows."

*** 

Liam had been on a lot of stages playing bass in the orchestra and jazz band, but something about this one was different. Maybe it was the aged boards that creaked as he walked, or the yards of velvet curtains that swayed gently for no reason. He didn't know, but there was definitely a feeling in the air, like ancient entertainers still hovered overhead, waiting for their turn in the spotlight.

"Hey, guys. Look what I found." Connor emerged from behind the curtain, dragging an old stand-up microphone.

Sarah gasped. "That's a Velocity ribbon!" She rushed over to study it more closely.

"Uh . . . okay," Connor said. "Is that a good thing?"

"This was true innovation during the big band era. All of the top studios used them."

"How do you know this stuff?" Connor asked.

"We have one just like it in the museum."

"Too bad the cord's frayed," Molly said.

"Doesn't matter. There's no electricity to the building anyway." David studied the mic. "Cool piece, though."

"Sarah, sing something. I'm going to do a video," Liam said.

"No way. I don't sing in front of people."

"It's okay, we're not people. We're your friends," Connor encouraged. "You sing and I'll air-guitar."

Sarah sighed but stepped behind the mic. "What should I sing?"

"How about 'Jail House Rock,'" Liam suggested.

"Elvis Presley? Really?"

The first few notes were strained, but it didn't take her long to get into the tune. Pretty soon, Molly joined them pretending to play a piano, and David sat on the floor tapping out a rhythm on the boards. Liam caught it all on the video, and when they stopped, he thought he heard quiet applause. He spun around.

"Did you guys hear something, just now?"

"Nope," Molly said.

"Like what?" Connor asked.

Liam stared out across the seats, expecting to see someone in the audience. There was no one there, but he rubbed a hand where the hairs on the back of his neck crawled. The creep factor of the building had amped up.

"It's getting dark. We should get back to the control room and set up for the night."

# CHAPTER ELEVEN

**M**olly sank to one of the blankets layered on the dusty floor of the control room.

"That was really fun. Sarah, you are such a great singer."

"Oh, thanks, Molly. My moms say the same thing. I really love it, but I get nervous singing in front of people. My throat closes up and my voice gets all squeaky." Sarah smiled. "Tonight was different, though. You're going to think this is really weird, but it was almost as if the building came alive a little bit when we were on stage goofing around. I think it really liked that we pretended to play and sing that old Elvis Presley song."

"It doesn't sound weird to me," Liam said. "I felt the same thing."

"That's crazy," Connor said. "Buildings don't have feelings."

"Do you think there're ghosts here?" Molly asked, looking over her shoulder.

"There is no scientific evidence that proves ghosts exist," David said.

"A few weeks ago, I would've agreed with you. Now, not so much. I know firsthand, so to speak, that strange things can happen, so maybe ghosts can too."

"Cora said that everything has energy, so why can't an old building have feelings?" Molly asked. She pulled the crystal from Cora out of her pocket and set it on the blanket. "This is moonstone. I googled it. Besides being a stone of inner growth and strength, it will help me develop my intuition."

"Yeah. I did a bunch of research online, too. Cora gave me a garnet. It's supposed to give me extra energy, courage and bring in adventure. I wonder how she knew that I like adventures?" Connor said. "Anyway, the next time we go to Cora's, I'm going to get a bunch more."

"I hope she has one that can make you smarter." Sarah grinned.

"Ha ha. Very funny."

Liam thought about the piece of sunstone in his pocket. He thought the gold-colored sparkly stone was beautiful and had researched its properties online. It was a stone of leadership, which he didn't think applied to him, but it did seem to energize him in some way. "Let's eat and talk about tomorrow's plan."

"Good idea. I'm starving," Connor said.

Molly fished the food out of her backpack and passed Liam's sandwich to him with a bag of chips. "What did you guys bring?"

"PB&J. Same as you," Sarah said, handing a sandwich to David.

"Oh man! You're all so boring." Connor zipped open his backpack. "Zingers, Twinkies, and Red Vines. I also have a can of Coke in here somewhere." He dug around for a moment, then pulled it out with a triumphant "Yes!"

Sarah took a bite of sandwich and glanced at the notebook in her lap. "Based on the bus times and the distance between locations, we'll have to hurry. We've got time to go to the record shop and the fire station. If we find out where Greg Ortman lives and go there, it'll be tight."

"I'm not sure what information we'll get from the shop. They might not keep track of who all brings in records," Molly said.

"Unless the guy's a regular," Connor said. "There're lots of people who buy and sell albums. Even if there aren't any official records, they may know him."

"Yeah, but what do we do?" Liam asked. "Walk in and say we have a record signed by a guy named Greg Ortman, and we'd really like to meet him?"

"What if we said there was a picture left in the album and we wanted to get it back to him?" Sarah suggested.

"That's perfect." Connor smiled.

"The only problem is we don't have a picture," Molly said.

David shrugged. "Just tell them you left it at home."

"Clever kid," Connor whispered. Liam nodded.

"Okay, we start at the record store and then what?" Liam asked.

"According to the map, it's only four blocks to the fire station," Sarah said.

"Okay, depending on what we get at the record store, we can go to the fire station. But if he's not there, then we're sunk," Connor said.

"So, we have a plan at the record store, but what about the fire station?"

"We could always use the same story," Sarah said.

"What do we say when he asks what the picture is of?"

"No problem. We'll tell him it's a picture of a girl in a blue tie-dye shirt. That way we can see if he gets upset or excited. Depending on his reaction, we can ask him who the girl is . . . or not."

"That could work," Liam said. "Let's hit the hay. Big day tomorrow."

They all mumbled agreement, then shuffled around with blankets and backpacks, trying to get comfortable.

Liam flicked off the light on his smartphone.

"Do you think we'll find him?" Connor quiet voice came out of the darkness.

"I don't know," Liam said. "But since I've been having these crazy visions, my life has been righteously messed up. It's nice to have friends to help me figure it all out. So, thanks."

A chorus of "you're welcomes" and one "no prob, dude" answered.

*** 

The music mingled with Liam's dream, but the sound of his friends rustling their blankets woke him fully. *Is that David's iPhone?* Liam sat up. Sarah stood at the window, looking down into the theatre. He stepped around Connor to stand on her other side. "What is it?"

"You hear it too?" she asked.

He nodded. "Sounds like jazz. Faint. Is it David's music? First Friday?"

"Nope. I think it's coming from the stage."

"The stage?" Connor asked. "Is someone else in the building?"

"There's probably a killer living here." Molly looked over her shoulder as if a knife-wielding maniac would leap into the room at any second. "He's just waiting for the right time to come in here and slash us to bits."

Liam looked at her. "Mom's murder mystery show, right?"

"Well . . . yeah. But it could be true."

Abruptly, the music stopped and the darkness in the auditorium was stabbed by a narrow beam of light.

"Someone's here!" Liam whispered. He ducked, pulling the others down with him.

"Oh no," Molly said. "What are we going to do?"

"We're going to sit right here and see what happens," Sarah said.

"She's right," Liam added. "No one will know we're here if we keep quiet."

"I'm going to see if I can tell who it is," Connor said, getting to his knees.

"Me too," Liam said.

"No! Don't," Sarah said, but it was too late. Liam and Connor were already on their knees, peering out the glass. She sighed and got up to look, too.

"There's two of them," Connor whispered. "They're going behind the stage."

The dark figures followed the bouncing beam until they disappeared behind the curtains. After a few minutes, the light returned and tracked back toward the big double doors. For a moment, the two stood, shrouded silhouettes against the wooden backdrop. Their heads bent together in conversation, and then the white hand of the larger figure shot out and gripped the other's shoulder. The timbre of a raised voice came through the glass. Liam couldn't make out the words, but the anger was clear. Molly choked, jerking back. The bang of her water bottle against the boards sounded like the roar of a cannon. The drama at the door stopped and the beam flashed around the auditorium. The friends all dropped to the floor.

Molly started to say something, but Liam put a finger to his lips. He barely breathed, listening for the squeak of the stair risers. When he heard only silence, he relaxed. Slowly, he craned his neck up to look out the window. The auditorium was empty.

Liam let out the breath he'd been holding and collapsed onto his blanket. He rubbed a hand over his heart, hoping to calm its panicked gallop.

"Oh my gosh," Sarah said. "That was close."

"That was pretty weird," Connor said. "I wonder what they were doing behind the stage?"

"Who do you think it was?" Molly asked.

"No idea," Liam said. "I'm just glad they left. I'm not sure if it's possible, but I'm going to try to get some sleep." He stretched out and pulled the blanket up to his chin, exposing his sock-clad feet and lower legs to the chilly air. The building creaked, settling around him, almost as if it were relaxing after the intrusion. Rustling in the corners turned his mind to Molly's stories of bizarre creatures and murder. His skin tingled in anticipation of a cold, clammy hand closing around his ankle. Mentally he rolled his eyes. *What a moron!* But he turned onto his side and pulled his legs up under the blanket. In the last few weeks, he'd seen the impossible turn into something quite real.

# CHAPTER TWELVE

L iam was already awake when the alarm on his phone pinged quietly. He nudged Connor. "Wake up. We gotta get the bus."

Connor just groaned, so Liam reached over to tap Molly on the shoulder.

"I'm awake," she said.

Sarah rolled off the pile of blankets she'd smashed into a cozy nest. "That was quite a night, huh?"

Liam nodded and poked Connor again. "Let's go. Get up."

Connor groaned and rolled over, finally getting up on all fours. Liam pulled energy bars out of his backpack and passed them around with small bottles of water. "This is it for food unless we have time to grab a bite in Kenosha."

"Wow, thanks, Liam," Sarah said. "I ate all of my PB&J last night."

"Hah," Connor said. "I've still got one pack of Twinkies left. I'll share."

Sarah made a face. "I'd rather starve."

"Okay. Suit yourself." Connor zipped up his backpack. "You don't know what you're missing."

"Ready to hit the road?"

Liam nudged Connor and stuck his hand out, palm down. Connor grinned and laid his on top, Molly placed hers on Connor's, and David followed suit. They all looked at Sarah, expectantly.

"Oh, whatever." She sighed and set her hand on top of the pile.

"Greg Ortman," they said in unison.

"Not quite the cheer I was hoping for, but it's a start," Connor said, and patted Liam on the back. "Today, we find our guy."

"I sure hope you're right," Liam said.

The only change in the office from the day before was the trail of their footprints in the thick dust on the floor. Liam opened the door just enough to peer out and make sure the coast was clear. Nothing greeted him but early morning light and birdsong, so he eased out onto the landing. The others followed and huddled for a moment, looking down at the ladder, which had returned to its original spot.

"How do we get down?" Molly asked.

"It's spring-loaded," David said. "Get on and it'll go down."

"Cool," Connor said. "I'll go first." He stepped onto the top rung and the ladder shot down to the ground, landing with a clank. "Whoa, that was awesome!"

"Spring's rusty," David said. "Don't get off or it'll come back up."

Hurrying, Sarah climbed onto the ladder and the others followed. When David was almost to the bottom, Liam reached back to shut the door. Before he could touch it, the door snicked shut and he thought he heard the sound of a deadbolt sliding into place. He didn't remember a lock on the inside of the door but just shrugged. The strange was quickly becoming the normal in his world. By the time he got to the bottom of the ladder, Connor was waist-deep in the bushes.

"Our bikes are gone."

"What?" Liam threw down his duffle and thrashed into the brush. *No, no no! How could they not be here?* The perpetual headache reared with fierce intensity, sharp hooves pummeling his temple. The image of the tie-dye shirt girl emerged, front and center, an accusing finger thrust out.

"Looking for these, boys and girls?"

Liam turned at the sound of Brandon's nasally whine. The bully and his pals held hostage the group's only means of transportation. Liam pushed out of the bushes and into the scrubby yard.

"Give us back the bikes, Brandon."

"Oh look. It's Lurch, the Hobbit, and his posse of pipsqueaks. Are you talking about these?" Brandon patted the seat of Liam's Pinnacle. "We found them in the bushes this morning. Figured you didn't want them anymore."

Out of the corner of his eye, Liam saw David pick up a dead branch. The kid did look menacing in his dark clothes and cap pulled low over his face. The others followed David's lead, but Liam thought he'd try reason first. He took a step forward. His friends flanked him.

"Just give 'em here and no harm done."

"Why would we do that?"

"Because there's five of us and only three of you." Connor slapped his branch against his palm.

"Ooh." Brandon grinned at his friends. "Are we scared?"

"I am, Brandon. I'm really, really scared," Kaylee giggled. Dylan only snickered.

Liam advanced another step. "I'm not kidding around here, Brandon. Those are our bikes and we want them back. We need them."

"Yeah? For what?"

He'd known Brandon since they were kids, and the boy had always had it in for him. It only got worse as they got older. There was no way he was going to tell Brandon they were going to Kenosha, but he needed some explanation. Liam held his hands out to his sides. "Come on, Brandon. We're just going biking."

"You want 'em? Come and get 'em."

Liam cringed at the smirk on Brandon's face.

"I think we can take them," Connor whispered.

*Is this going to end up in a fistfight?* Liam hoped not, but one way or the other, he was going to Kenosha today. Liam met Brandon's hard stare with a determined look of his own and stooped to pick up a branch. Suddenly, Brandon's eyes shifted to a spot over Liam's shoulder. His face turned ash-white. He uttered a gasping squeak and staggered back a step.

Liam spun around, expecting to see a cop, or maybe Brandon's dad, but all he saw was a quick movement in the upper window of the Orpheum.

He turned back to Brandon in time to see the boy throw down the bike he was holding and run. The other two gaped after him, then followed, leaving all of the bikes behind.

"I guess he didn't like the odds," Connor said.

"Yeah," Liam said, looking back at the façade of the old theatre. "I guess he didn't."

*** 

There were a surprising number of people on the bus for that early on a Saturday morning. Liam kept the hood up on his jacket and told the others to do the same.

"We don't want to be recognized."

When the bus finally pulled into the stop near the Kenosha town square, Liam could see the river walk just a half block away. Shops and restaurants lined the street, which was already alive with people wandering the weekly farmers' market.

They filed off the bus and collected their bikes from the rack. Liam led them to a quiet corner across from one of the market booths.

"Looks like we just head north from here six blocks and take a left," Sarah said, pointing to the map on Liam's phone.

They found the record store and parked their bikes in a rack outside. Liam pulled off his backpack and fished out the album.

"So, who's doing the talking?"

"I think Connor should do it," Sarah said. "It's his record, and that'll make the story sound more believable."

"Okay," Connor said. "I'll talk here and then we can figure out who gets the fire station."

Block Street Records was a small shop, long and narrow with bins full of used albums and records lining the walls. Just inside the door was a checkout desk with concert posters and T-shirts pinned behind it.

"Wow! This place is awesome," Connor said.

Sarah nudged him. "Stay focused. We don't have time to gawk."

"Yeah, yeah. Okay." He walked over to the counter.

The clerk was a young woman with a large tattoo across her chest and trailing down her arms. A thin chain swung from her nose ring to a single hoop in her left ear. Jet-black hair hung in dreadlocks with one stripe of red braid across the front. "Hey. You need help?"

"Well, kind of," Connor said. "My uncle bought this record here and it has a name on it. Do you know this guy? We're trying to find him."

"Why?" The girl looked from Connor to the others.

"Um . . . We found a picture in the album sleeve and just thought he may want it back. It looks, uh . . . personal."

"That's weird. We go through everything before we put it out for sale. Must have missed that. Let's see the name again."

Connor held the album out to her. She studied the writing for a moment, then shook her head. "Nope. Don't know him. Can I see the picture? Maybe I'll recognize the face."

"Well, the problem is I forgot to bring the photo with me, but he's not in it. It's a picture of a girl. She's wearing a blue tie-dye T-shirt."

"Without the photo, I don't think I'm going to be much help. Did you google the name? Try the phone book?"

"That's our next step; we just thought someone here might know him."

"Sorry, I wish I could help. If you don't find him, you could always bring the photo back here. I can put it on the board to see if someone claims it." She pointed to a corkboard riddled with notices for all kinds of events, lost pets, and items for sale.

Connor thanked her and they trailed out of the shop.

"Strike one," Liam said.

"What a cool shop, though. We should come back and look around."

"Forget the store." Liam checked his watch. "We've gotta get to the fire station or we'll run out of time."

***

They stopped their bikes across the street from a plain two-story redbrick building. One large, black garage door was closed, and painted on the front in gold letters was *KFD #3*. The other door was open to a large bay where a glistening red engine sat. Two men in khaki pants and dark shirts stood by the open front passenger door.

"Okay. Who's talking here?" Connor asked.

"It should be Molly," David said.

Molly's eyes widened. "I don't know."

"He's right," Sarah agreed. "Nobody would suspect her of anything."

"Uh . . . thanks, I guess." She smiled tentatively at Sarah. "Okay, I'll . . . uh . . . do it."

"Here we go."

They walked their bikes across the street and leaned them against the brick wall. Liam took the record from his pack and held it out to Molly.

"You'll be fine. You know what to say, and we'll be with you."

She nodded, rubbed her palms on her jeans, then took the album. "I've got this."

They went through the open bay door and the two men inside turned to them. One was young and the other seemed much older.

"Hey, kids," the older man said. "I'm Captain Racine. What can I do you for?"

The captain was about the same height as Liam, but his arms and chest were huge. He looked like he could pick up a car. When the man's question was answered with silence, Liam glanced at Molly. She stared up at the man, mouth open but unable to speak. Before he could do anything, Sarah stepped forward.

"Hello, sir. We are wondering if you can help us."

"Maybe. What do you need?" The captain lowered his head, looking at them over his sunglasses.

"We're trying to find the original owner of this album." Sarah took the record from Molly and held it out. "This was bought at Block Street Records. It has the name Greg Ortman written on it. We found a picture in the album sleeve and want to return it to Mr. Ortman. We tried the record store first, but they didn't know who he was. Google says there's a man by that name who is a firefighter. So . . . do you know him?"

The two firemen exchanged a long look, then turned suspicious eyes on Sarah. Finally, the younger one shook his head. "Sorry, kids, can't help ya."

"But . . . does he work here?"

The younger man glanced at Captain Racine and the captain gave a subtle nod.

"Yeah, but Ortman's off today. He won't be back on until Monday. You can leave the picture here and we'll make sure he gets it."

"Well, the problem is, we forgot the picture, and we really don't know if he is the right Greg Ortman. We found a couple on Google," Liam said.

"Well, I don't know what to tell you."

"I don't suppose you could call him and see if he'll come and talk to us?" Liam asked.

"Or tell us where he lives," Sarah said quickly.

"No, I don't think so, but nice try."

Out of the corner of his eye, Liam saw Connor slide away and slip through the door leading into the firehouse. Quickly, he stepped toward the fire engine. He grasped the door handle and swung up on the running board. "What a cool engine. Can I look inside?"

"Hey, get off of there." The younger fireman grabbed Liam by the sleeve of his sweatshirt and tugged.

Liam made a big show of losing his balance, falling against the man and then to the ground. Captain Racine strode over and picked Liam up like he weighed nothing at all. Still holding tightly to his arms, the man leaned in until they were nose to nose.

"Do not touch city property without permission. Understand?" He stared at Liam a moment longer, then released him. He looked over at the others. "Wait a second. Where's the kid with the long hair?"

"Uh, who?" Liam stalled for time.

"There was another kid with you. Where'd he go?" When Liam shrugged, the captain turned to the younger man. "Keep an eye on them, Jack." He headed for the door where Connor had disappeared.

"Time to go."

David's whisper over his shoulder echoed Liam's own thoughts, and he started to back away toward the bikes.

"Hey, hold up." The fireman started toward them.

They turned and ran. Liam could hear the heavy footsteps coming behind them and was glad they didn't have far to go.

"Where's Connor?" Sarah hissed as she pulled her bike away from the wall.

Liam quickly took the album from her and shoved it into his pack. "Don't talk, just ride." He turned away, grabbed Connor's bike by the handlebars and mounted his own.

As they rounded the side of the building, Connor banged out of a side door and ran toward them. He leaped onto his bike and they pedaled away as if a pack of vicious dogs were after them.

# CHAPTER THIRTEEN

L iam led them several blocks from the fire station and stopped.

"Whew, that was close." Molly wiped sweat off her cheek.

Sarah let her bike fall and stomped over to Connor. "What were you doing? We almost got into real trouble."

"Yeah, but I got this." Connor pulled a piece of white paper from his pocket.

"What is it?"

"A list of all the firemen at the station with their phone numbers . . . and addresses."

"Seriously?" Sarah snatched the paper from him. "Look at this. Greg Ortman is right here."

"Way to go, Connor." Liam slapped him on the back.

"Well, I didn't think that guy was going to tell us anything, so I figured . . ."

"Did you see the look they gave each other? It was as if they knew something fishy about Greg Ortman."

"Something like maybe they know he's a murderer?" Molly squeaked.

"Oh, come on," Sarah said. "You're getting paranoid. Besides, we still don't know if this is the right guy."

"Maybe we shouldn't go to his house?" Molly said. "We could always come back to the station when he's working. He wouldn't try to grab us with other firefighters there."

"It's too late for that. They would probably kick us out as soon as they saw us."

"Yeah, or call the cops on us," Connor said.

"You can go home if you want to, but I'm going to the house." Liam took the paper from Sarah. "I've come too far not to finish this and figure out what the girl wants. I will never get my life back if I don't."

"I agree," Connor said. "Let's do this thing."

"Oh man," Molly sighed. "I sure hope you know what you're doing."

*Me too*, Liam thought and typed the address on the paper into the map app on his phone.

They were almost there when Liam braked suddenly. The others shot past him, but he didn't pay any attention. He'd had some very odd experiences in just a few weeks. His life had totally changed and he'd come to accept a gift he never wanted. But what he saw on the hillside ramped up the awesomeness of what that really meant.

"Dude," Connor said when they'd pedaled back to where Liam was stopped. "Come on. We gotta get going."

Liam didn't answer. He simply pointed to a distant building perched on a small hill.

"Yeah, so?" Connor asked.

Liam pulled the sketch he'd made of the building out of his backpack and held it up. "It's the one I saw in my vision."

Sarah gasped. "It's exactly the same."

"Uh huh." Liam nodded. "This is definitely the right Greg Ortman."

*** 

As they turned onto Olive Street, Liam stopped his bike and the others pulled up beside him.

"His house will be on the left side. Let's go up the right and do a drive-by to scout it out."

As they drew closer, Liam saw a man washing a black pickup truck in what he calculated would be Greg Ortman's driveway. Liam turned his bike onto the sidewalk and stopped.

"That may be him right there." Connor pointed.

Liam grabbed Connor's arm and shoved it down. "Don't."

Sarah glanced over. "The shirt he's wearing looks like the one Captain Racine had on."

Liam took a deep breath, stuck his hand in his pocket and touched the crystal. It was as if he could feel the pulse of it, and it gave him the added strength he needed to finish this up.

"Okay, guys, are you ready for this? I'll do the talking."

"You sure?" Sarah asked.

"No worries, Sarah. He's got this. Right, Liam?" Connor said.

Liam nodded. He pushed his bike across the street and down the sidewalk. The others flanked him. Liam was glad the man was outside and that he didn't have to ring the doorbell.

He felt a trickle of sweat sneak down the back of his neck and wiped it away. He was resolved to help the girl in the tie-dye shirt, but his hands still shook as he pulled the record out of his pack.

The man was bent over, scrubbing the tire rims with a brush. He didn't seem to notice they were there.

Liam cleared his throat. Still nothing.

"Excuse me, sir," he said and touched him on the shoulder.

The man jumped and whirled around, spraying water and soap over the kids. "Oh, wow. Sorry about that. You startled me," he said, with a chuckle. "Sometimes I get in the zone when I'm washing my truck."

Liam smiled and swiped at the beads of water that had landed on his sweatshirt. "Are you Greg Ortman?"

The man hesitated for a moment, then nodded. "Can I help you with something?"

"My name is Liam. This is my sister, Molly, and my friends Connor, Sarah, and David. We're sorry to bother you, but is this your record?"

The man studied the album cover for a moment, then looked up at Liam, a puzzled look on his face. "Uh . . . yes, or I should say it was. I sold it down at the record store about a year ago. Why?"

"My uncle bought it for my birthday," Connor said.

"That's nice. It's a great album. I must have played it hundreds of times when I was your age."

Liam nodded. He was struggling with how to bring up the girl in the blue tie-dye shirt. "Does this record have any special meaning for you? Or did anything happen while you were listening to it?"

Ortman's eyes narrowed. "That's an odd question."

"Does a girl wearing a blue tie-dye shirt mean anything to you?" Sarah blurted out.

"Look," he said. "I don't know what you're up to, but the answer is no. I don't know any girl like that."

"We're not up to anything, honest," Connor jumped in. "When I got the album, there was a picture of a girl wearing a blue tie-dye shirt tucked into the sleeve. We thought you might know who she is. We want to return the picture to the owner."

Greg ran a damp hand through his hair and sighed. "To be honest, kids, I got the record from my dad. But I don't remember seeing a photo. Maybe someone else had the album before your uncle bought it?"

Liam glanced over his shoulder at the factory sitting on the hill. "No, I don't think so." He was sure this was the right man.

"How did you know I used to own the album? I don't think the store keeps records like that. If they do, they wouldn't give out the information."

Liam pointed to the name inked in the corner of the album cover. Greg traced it gently.

"So, you tracked me down with just this? You realize that's a little creepy, right?"

Liam felt his face burn hot with embarrassment. The man didn't know the half of it. "Yes. I guess it is. It's just that we felt it was important."

"Because of this supposed photo that you found?"

"Uh-huh," Liam said.

"Okay," Greg nodded as if coming to a decision. "That's my dad's writing. We're both Greg Ortman, though our middle names are different. He was funny about writing his name on stuff—still is, actually. I guess you could talk to him about it if you want to. He's in the back."

*There was another Greg Ortman! Here!* "Thanks, that would be great."

The man motioned for them to follow him.

Liam started forward, but Molly grabbed his arm. "Are you crazy? We don't know this man at all. I know we were just kidding about him being a murderer, but what if—"

"Molly, calm down," Connor said. "This guy is a fireman. And, anyway, we're not going into the house, just in the back."

"He's right, Molly," Sarah said. "We'll be fine."

"Okay. But I'm going on record that this is officially insane."

"Yeah. Cool, isn't it?" Connor said, wiggling his brows up and down.

They followed Greg along the side of the house and into a large backyard. An elderly man sat on a bucket, pruning a flowering bush. He wore jeans and a tan button-down shirt. A large-brimmed brown hat shaded his face and neck.

"Hey, Dad," Greg said. "These kids have something that may interest you."

"Well, I hope it's a green thumb because I sure could use it." His chuckle was deep and raspy. He winced as he rose from his seat.

"Hello, sir." Liam stepped forward and introduced everyone. "We think this used to be yours."

The man pulled off his gloves and reached for the album. His face crinkled in pleasure when he saw the cover. "Ah yes, a blast from the past." He opened it reverently. "The Allman Brothers were one of my favorites."

The younger Greg looked at Liam and smiled. "He gave me a big stack of records when I was around your age. When my wife and I cleaned out the garage, I found them and decided to sell them. I guess I should've checked with Dad first."

The elder Mr. Ortman looked up at his son. "I got this album about six months after your mom and I got married. We'd just moved into our first apartment and I was working at the Ford dealership." His eyes teared up as he brushed his hand over the cover. "It's funny, but I remember the day so clearly. It was the first brand-new record I ever bought. All of the others I had up until then were used or given to me. I was beside-myself excited. Came right home and put it on the turntable. I was married to the girl of my dreams, had a good job and could buy something I wanted. I felt like a real adult, king of the world."

He chuckled and looked back up at his son. "I was sitting there, listening to the music, having a moment . . . you know. Your mom comes in crying and all upset. At first, I got a little annoyed, and then when she couldn't stop crying, I got scared. I thought maybe something was really wrong. Finally, she told me she just found out she was pregnant . . . with you. We were both so happy and terrified all at the same time. We didn't know anything about raising a kid, but we knew we loved each other." He shook his head and smiled. "Next to the day you were born, had to be one of the best days of my life."

Greg slung an arm around his father's shoulders. "I miss her every day."

"Me too." His father knuckled away tears.

"Do you happen to remember what she was wearing that day?" Liam asked.

"I sure do. This ugly blue tie-dye T-shirt. She loved it and wore it through her pregnancy. The darn thing got so stretched out, she couldn't wear it once Greg was born. She kept it, though. I remember tossing it in the pile for the Goodwill when I went through her things. Had to have been thirty years old." Mr. Ortman held out the record to Liam. "Thank you for showing this to me. You kids made my day."

Liam smiled. They had done a good thing by finding this man. He reached out and touched the album and the two Greg Ortmans vanished. The sense of accomplishment he'd just felt evaporated, replaced with terror that wasn't his own. The girl loomed, huge and intense. She sobbed and shook her head. A groan caught in his throat. He squeezed his eyes shut against the dizziness and reeled back into Connor.

"Uh-oh. It's happening again," Connor said, catching Liam around the arm.

Liam gripped Connor's sleeve, staring at him but seeing flames erupting from the decaying factory. Piercing, acrid smoke filled his nostrils. *Stop him!* the girl's words shrieked in his head.

Sarah rushed to grab Liam's other arm and they eased him to the ground. She knelt beside him. "What are you seeing, Liam? Can you tell me?"

He wanted to tell her, but the words clenched in his throat. Pain rattled when he shook his head.

"What's going on? Is he all right?" Mr. Ortman asked.

"Yes, he'll be okay in a minute. Probably just dehydrated. Could you get him some water, please?" Connor asked.

"Of course."

"Let me see him. He may need the medics." Greg squatted down just as his cell phone rang.

A thick veil of nothingness separated Liam from the others. Through it he heard muffled voices and then the sharp ring of a phone. The sensation sliced across his skin. When Greg answered it, Liam's mouth gaped in a silent scream. What the girl had been trying to tell him clicked into place. He wasn't supposed to just *find* Greg Ortman—he was supposed to *save* him. Liam struggled to sit up.

"No!" The word gargled out weakly. He gritted his teeth and opened his eyes.

"Yeah, no problem. I'll be out front," Greg said into the phone.

Liam grabbed the front of Greg's T-shirt. "Don't. You can't."

"What are you doing? Let go." Greg jerked free and strode toward the gate.

Liam heard the siren in the distance and saw a plume of smoke on the hill. *The factory.* It was on fire. He raced after Greg. The engine pulled to the curb as they rounded the corner of the house. Captain Racine and the other firefighter were in the cab.

Liam stepped in front of Greg. "Don't. You can't go. It's not safe." Greg tried to push him aside, but Liam refused to move.

"Listen, I don't know what's wrong with you, but I've got to go. There's an emergency."

Behind him, Liam heard the truck doors open.

"Hey, those are the kids from the station. What're they doing here?"

Greg looked from his captain to Liam. "What are you talking about?"

"They came by the station. Said they wanted to return a picture to you. That one stole our roster." Captain Racine pointed at Connor.

Greg's face contorted in anger. "What?"

"Mr. Ortman," Liam started, but the man sliced his hand through the air to cut him off.

"You stay put, you hear me? I'll deal with you when I get back."

"No." Liam knew he couldn't let the tie-dye girl's son leave. "I won't let you." He ran to the cab of the fire engine and threw himself inside, slamming the doors and punching the lock button.

The surprised looks on the firefighters' faces would've been funny if Liam hadn't felt so desperate. He watched as the captain searched his pockets for the keys. Liam knew that was a waste of time because they were dangling from the ignition. Captain Racine gave up and the three of them pummeled the windows, shouting at him to open up. Liam shook his head, knowing he would be grounded for the rest of his life, never get into a music college, much less be selected for the honors program. He'd probably only play his music on street corners and die a horrible death all alone, but at least he would have saved one man. And maybe the tie-dye girl would leave him alone now.

Captain Racine moved to the back of the engine and Liam heard the compartment doors opening. He jumped when the man's angry face appeared in the window. The captain held up a key for Liam to see. Then the door flew open. Liam's arm was gripped in an iron fist and he was jerked from the cab.

"Do not move from this spot," the captain growled.

The three firemen leaped into the engine and tore out of the driveway.

The tie-dye girl keened, screaming, *No! No! No!* The pain-sound lashed through Liam's head. He watched the truck race away and knew he'd failed her.

Through bleary eyes, Liam saw the firetruck disappear around the corner. It wouldn't take them long to reach the paved road snaking up to the blazing factory. When he saw the straight line of power poles marching up the hill, he knew what he had to do.

"Come on," he shouted to his friends and ran toward the bikes. They could beat the truck to the fire if they took the pole line up the hill.

They reached the base of the trail quickly. Liam didn't hesitate. His legs churned and the bike flew up the cleared path as if powered by twin jet packs. He sailed over the crest with David's BMX close behind, the others strung out in a line. Liam slid to a stop on the road. Briefly, he stared at the inferno of the factory, heat searing his face and ash falling around him, then turned toward the approaching trucks.

The others joined him, forming a barrier of bikes and kids. Sirens screamed! Horns blared! The faces of the three firemen loomed in the windshield, tense with determination. Greg Ortman leaned out the window, shouted at them to move. Liam cringed as the engine barreled down. He kept one hand on his bike, the other clasped around the stone in his pocket. When he thought the engine would surely smash them to pulp, the brakes squealed and the truck fishtailed to a halt. The three men tumbled out.

A thunderclap of explosion banged into him. The force tossed him to the ground and he skidded on face, hands and knees across the pavement. Chunks of brick, plaster, and shards of glass showered around him. Just like in the vision of the school desk.

Liam lay on the ground, arms sheltering his head from the storm of debris. *Molly, Connor, Sarah and David. Are they all right?* He struggled to his hands and knees. Tried to shake the ringing from his ears.

"Whoa, whoa, whoa. Stay down, son." A medic squatted next to him.

"My friends! I need to get to them."

The man put his hands on Liam's shoulders, gently helped him to a sitting position. "It's okay. They're being looked after."

Liam heard the man through the fog, but in his vision, the tie-dye girl danced. She whooped, did a little spin and giggled. Her gentle *Thank you!* was like a caress to his aching head. She blew him a kiss and disappeared with a pop.

The others joined him, sitting together on the asphalt.

"We did it. We saved Greg Ortman," Liam said.

"Woo-hoo!" Connor fist-bumped with the others, then Liam. "Dude, that was totally awesome!"

"Where are your parents, kids?" the paramedic asked. "What are you doing here?"

Liam looked at the medics, then at his friends and sister.

"He wants to know what we're doing here," he said, and couldn't stop the laughter that tumbled out of him.

***

Liam could hear only half of Mr. Ortman's conversation with his dad and it didn't sound that good. Mr. Ortman kept repeating that they were all right, but it was as if his dad wasn't listening. Liam exchanged a look with his sister.

"We are so dead," he said.

"Yeah. No more volleyball for me this season. But that was so awesome, it was worth it."

"It really was," Connor agreed. He looked at Liam. "Dude, you were right. How crazy is that?"

"Yeah, I guess so," Liam said, a spark of wonder in his eyes. A man's life had been saved because of a vision he had. He had to think about what that meant for the future.

"Now what?" Connor said.

"Now what, what?" Liam asked. "We'll probably all be grounded until graduation. Hopefully I won't get kicked out of orchestra. But for sure I can kiss the honors performance goodbye."

"I know that. I may never get to leave the house again except to go to school, but what I mean is, what do we do next with all of this . . . you know?"

"I don't know." Liam stared at his friends but looked inward. This gift had put him on a path he'd never imagined for himself. It felt good, *right*, and he wanted to know more, to do more. "I guess I use this gift to help people."

"Heck yeah," Molly said.

"Remember when I said we need a name, like for a club?"

"Oh, Connor," Sarah said. "Not that again. Don't you think it's a bit childish?"

"Well, yeah, maybe, but I've been thinking about it," Connor said. "Since we all live on Mud Street, how about we call ourselves the Amazing Mud Street Detective Agency."

"No, that sounds silly," Molly laughed.

"How about the Mud Street Five?" Liam said.

"Or how about this: the Mud Street Marvelous Five!" Connor said.

"Marvelous? Amazing?" Sarah rolled her eyes. "We're just kids, not cool and not nerdy. Just kids with weird lives. David and I have two moms. You and Molly have two families. Connor is, well . . . Connor. We're more misfits than marvelous."

"She has a point," Connor said. "We *are* a bit anomalous."

"Anomalous? Where did you hear that word?" Liam asked.

"My mom," Connor snickered. "She does crossword puzzles and is always trying to expand her vocabulary. It was the word of the day on Friday. It means abnormal . . . different. I think it fits, don't you?"

"Yup," Liam laughed. "I guess we're the Mud Street Misfits!"

\*\*\*

As Liam rode with Molly into Ashford Park, he spotted his friends over by the fountain. Connor was practicing balancing on his bike without moving and Sarah was reading a book.

David wore his ever-present headphones and bobbed his head to music.

"Finally, the first official meeting of the Mud Street Misfits can begin," Connor said, tossing down his bike and taking a place at the table.

"I can't believe we only got grounded for a week!" Sarah said.

"No kidding," Molly said.

"Well, duh. We saved people's lives," Connor said. "We should be getting a medal."

"I don't need a medal." Liam dropped his backpack onto the picnic table and sat down. "I'm just glad everyone's alive."

"What happened to the tie-dye girl? Do you still see her?" Sarah asked.

Liam shook his head. "I actually got through an entire orchestra practice and did my demo vid for the honors program. I'll find out soon if I got accepted."

"Way cool, dude." Connor held up his hand for a high-five.

"Do you think you'll have more visions?" David pulled off his headphones.

"Don't know. Guess I'll just have to wait and see."

"I hope you do. Solving the mystery of the tie-dye girl was awesome. I wanna do it again," Connor said.

"I think we need to go back to Cora's and tell her what happened," Molly said.

"Yeah. She's gonna be blown away."

"Actually," Liam said with a smile, "I don't think she'll be too surprised."

"Really?" Sarah asked. "Why not?"

"She just kinda knew stuff."

"You think she's psychic, too?" Connor asked.

Liam nodded.

"Wow." Connor looked around like he was seeing the town for the first time. "I wonder how many other people in Ozark are psychic?"

"I would like to meet her and maybe get one of those stones," Sarah said.

"Me too." Molly turned her bike toward Main Street. "Let's go, guys. My allowance money is burning a hole in my pocket."

As they rode past the Orpheum Theatre, Liam skidded to a stop.

"What's all this?" he said, pointing to the orange barrels and yellow tape surrounding the building.

David rode up to a poster stapled to a wooden pole. "It says this is a demolition site."

"Oh no!" Sarah cried. "That creep, Mayor Scott, is determined to destroy every historic building in this town. Remember what happened to that old schoolhouse?" She gazed up at the building, then squinted at Liam. "Tear down this beautiful place? I don't think so. Not if the Mud Street Misfits have anything to say about it."

## ABOUT THE AUTHORS

*After long days working in an office, Brian spent many nights reading books and telling stories of adventures to his four children. Building off inspiration from his family, the stories became bigger and more animated and the request for stories became more frequent. Brian has always told his children to explore the world and chase their dreams. With encouragement and support from his family, Brian made the decision to follow one of his own dreams, writing down and sharing his stories with other Misfits!!*

*A Misfit herself, Beth's fascination with all things "woo-woo" goes back to her childhood where she spent many hours in fantasy worlds of her own creation. As an adult, knowing there was more to life than just what we see with our eyes, she began an exploration of these fascinating other realms. A love of writing and the desire to share her knowledge sparked the creation of many short stories. Now, Beth is excited to share her love of the unknown with a new generation of readers and fellow Misfits!!*